# Rush to the Heartland

# Rush to the Heartland

KELLY DIEHL YATES

RESOURCE *Publications* · Eugene, Oregon

RUSH TO THE HEARTLAND

Resource Publications
An Imprint of Wipf and Stock Publishers
199 W. 8th Ave., Suite 3
Eugene, OR 97401

www.wipfandstock.com

PAPERBACK ISBN: 978-1-6667-0277-4
HARDCOVER ISBN: 978-1-6667-0278-1
EBOOK ISBN: 978-1-6667-0279-8

05/17/21

Dedicated to Florence Virginia Grayson Barry, 1919–1998
My maternal grandmother
She taught me to love books.

# Contents

*Acknowledgements* | ix
*Preface* | xi
*Prologue* | xiii

**Part One: Tennessee**—February 1889
1    *The Dance* | 3
2    *The Outlaws* | 9
3    *The Fall* | 15
4    *Sally* | 20

**Part Two: Arkansas**—March, 1889
5    *Unforgiveness* | 31
6    *The Proposal* | 36
7    *Books* | 45
8    *Fort Smith* | 51
9    *Illness* | 64

**Part Three: Indian Territory**—March 1889
10   *Aenohe* | 71
11   *Wondering* | 83
12   *Planning* | 89

**Part Four: Oklahoma Territory**—March–April 1889
13   *The Town* | 95
14   *Jessie's Plan* | 108
15   *Speculating* | 113
16   *The Boomer Train* | 116

17  The Birth | 120

18  The Dilemma | 124

19  The Injury | 135

20  Jessie's Tale | 140

21  The Last Miles | 143

22  The Soddy | 145

23  Amos | 149

24  The Saloon | 151

25  The Journal | 156

26  Love in the Heartland | 164

Epilogue | 167

# Acknowledgements

A special thanks to the following people:

Brianna Yates-Grantz, my daughter, for editing.

Wanda Van Winkle, for editing.

Heather Clemmer, professor of History, Southern Nazarene University for her advice.

Chad Long, Oklahoma History teacher at Mustang (Oklahoma) High School, for his advice.

My husband Chris, daughter, Skyler, and my parents, Steve and Paula Diehl for always believing in me.

# *Preface*

WE HAVE A TARNISHED history. When my children attended an Oklahoma public school, April 22, "Land Run Day" was a celebration. The students dressed in pioneer garb and decorated their red wagons as prairie schooners and reenacted the infamous race. Now this has exited much of the curriculum, understandably so. We should not observe something that celebrates genocide. For instance, Oklahoma City Public Schools now celebrate an Oklahoma History Day that remembers all angles of the first Land Run, including the experience of Native Americans. With my Oklahoma Land Rush series of books, I would like to do the same: remember the Land Rush from all angles: the struggles of those who took the land, and those who lost the land.

On March 23, 1889, President William Henry Harrison, the ninth U. S. president, declared the 1.9 million-acre section of Indian Territory (now central Oklahoma) would be open for settlement at noon on April 22, 1889. Knowing they could claim a quarter section, 160 acres, under the Homestead Act of 1862, 50,000 land-starved pioneers flooded the territory and by a race, seized one of the final pieces of earth allotted to the Native Americans, and around 11,000 homesteads were claimed. After occupying and improving the land for five years, the settlers could claim a title. This was the first of five Land Runs: the next two took place in 1891, and the final two happened in 1893 and 1895. The Land Run of 1889 is the most famous, and often referred to as "The Land Run" even though there were four more.

The Land Runs happened in part due to the American belief in Manifest Destiny. Manifest Destiny, a phrase that originated in 1845, was a general cultural belief that God destined white Americans to settle the west until they reached the Pacific Ocean. However, critics today question this belief because it was used to justify the removal and genocide of Native Americans. I am one of these critics.

Therefore, it is not my intention to celebrate the Land Runs or Manifest Destiny with this book, but to tell a story of Americans who lived during this time. My characters are some of those 50,000 "Boomers" in 1889 who heard of a chance to get free land and they journeyed west; like so many others had done before them. Most never thought of the consequences of taking the land from the Native Americans, unless they encountered them. Even with an altercation, the settlers believed they had every right to the land.

As you will encounter in the story, only one person questions what they are doing, and it does not change their plans. Although her questioning influences one other person, this is as far as it goes. With this, I've tried to create a story that is as close to the historical events as possible. True to history, some of my characters hold deep prejudices against Native Americans.

The second book, *Division in the Heartland: The Town with No Men*, will tell the story of women who gained land in the fourth land run of September 16, 1893, and founded and occupied a town in which they allowed no men. It will attempt to demonstrate the struggle for human rights that the women of the nineteenth century led. Additionally, the third book, *Anguish in the Heartland: Aenohe's Story*, will document the struggle of Aenohe, a member of the Cheyenne tribe, whom the characters encounter on their journey to the Land Run. Therefore, together, the three books in the series will attempt to narrate a well-rounded history of the events of the late nineteenth century in what is now the state of Oklahoma.

# *Prologue*

## Guthrie, Oklahoma, July 22, 1989

"MEMAW, MEMAW!"

The cries of a sixteen-year-old girl woke Anne from her dreams. Never in her eighty years had the heat worn her out as it did these days. The air conditioning window unit in her old house on Harrison Street did little to fight the 110–degree July winds in Guthrie, Oklahoma.

Lizzie, her sixteen–year–old granddaughter, came walking into the room.

"Memaw, I bought you something!"

"Yes, child, what is it?"

"It's a shirt!"

Anne placed her glasses on the edge of her nose. She peered inside the white paper sack at a reddish–brown colored T-shirt. The shirt boasted, "Dyed in real Oklahoma red dirt."

"Well, well, they finally found some good use for that devilish dirt." She patted Lizzie on the shoulder. "Thank you, Lizzie. It's a lovely gift. Where's your mother?"

"In the car. She's coming."

Anne's daughter, Priscilla, took care of her aging mother. Without her care, Anne would be residing in the nursing home on Oklahoma Street instead of in her lifelong home.

Priscilla walked in a saw her mother on the recliner. "Oh, hello, Mama, has Lizzie spilled the beans about your gift already?" She noted Anne with the shirt in her lap.

Anne laughed–a hoarse chuckle. "I can't believe what they've done with this dirt! Why, I remember Mama scolding me a hundred times for wearing light–colored clothing outside. The red dirt doesn't come out, no matter how much you soak it in bleach, and here they are dyeing T–shirts in it."

"I would so love Lizzie to hear your stories about Grandma," said Priscilla.

"Well, why not?" Anne leaned back in her recliner, groaning about her arthritis. "I'll tell you about her journey to Indian Territory for the Land Run of 1889."

"Sit down, Lizzie Lou. I want Memaw to tell you about her mother, your great grandmother, Elizabeth."

"Grandma Elizabeth Louise, the one I was named after?"

"Yes, Lizzie."

"But she already has, Mom. I know all about her. She rode a train to Guthrie and then helped build the town."

"That's not exactly how it happened, dear," Anne said. "I think it's time for you to hear the whole story."

"Wait, wait, Mama, I have my video camera in the car. I want to record your story." Priscilla dashed out the door.

"Lizzie, dear, fetch my hairbrush from the bathroom cabinet, would you? I didn't know your mother was going to make a movie of me today."

A few minutes later, with the camera with a large VHS tape settled on its tripod, Anne began the familiar story. She held the reddish–brown T–shirt in her hands, rubbing it absently as she spoke.

"Elizabeth came to Oklahoma from Virginia."

"In a wagon train, Memaw?" Lizzie interrupted.

"A few people met together and decided to travel to Oklahoma in wagons. It wasn't a wagon train like you read about in your history books, with the long lines of Prairie Schooners."

"Sooner, like the Oklahoma Sooners?"

"No, a Schooner is a wagon, Lizzie Lou."

"I know that. I've had Oklahoma history. I just didn't know which one you meant. A Sooner was a person." But Elizabeth began to hum "Boomer Sooner" under her breath anyway.[1]

Then she asked, "Was Grandmother Elizabeth a Sooner?"

"No, but she had the opportunity to be one."

"Lizzie, why don't we let Memaw talk for a few minutes?" Priscilla said.

"Really, Prissy, I don't mind the questions."

"I know you don't, but I would like to get this story recorded."

Lizzie settled down at the foot of her grandmother's battered old recliner. She leaned back, her lids closing over her blue eyes. She scooped her long dark curls into a bun and wrapped the elastic band around it she always carried on her wrist. She wondered what it was like to live in 1889.

1. "Boomer Sooner" is the fight song of the University of Oklahoma Sooners football team.

*Part One*

# *Tennessee*

February 1889

# 1

# *The Dance*

Morning sounds filled the air as Elizabeth opened her eyes. The smell of morning coffee, eggs, and bacon drifted to her nose. She could hear Jessie and Emma, the two sisters with whom she traveled, whisper near her.

"I'm awake." She tried to pull herself to a sitting position.

"Now, you just stop that." Jessie turned toward Elizabeth, gently pushing her back onto the soft pile of worn quilts. The odor of Jessie's wad of tobacco met with Elizabeth's nose. Elizabeth grimaced, her hand moving to her pregnancy-stretched abdomen.

"We're n-not m-moving." Elizabeth whispered, her dry throat, irritated.

"Jeremiah gave you until noon to rest, and then we're pulling out. He said the horses could use the rest anyway. Ain't that just like menfolk? They fret more over dumb animals than womenfolk." Jessie snorted with disgust. A steady stream of tobacco shot from her mouth to the rocky, hard, almost frozen ground outside the wagon.

"Don't let them lose time on my account," Elizabeth said.

"What do you mean? With you in that condition, we can't move this wagon!" Jessie shifted the remainder of her wad to the other cheek. "The Doc told Jeremiah you must have been shocked by the holdup. He said you were a *delicate* little female. Of course, that made Jeremiah say he wished he would've left you behind. But since the holdup, we got to sit here and figure on how we're going to go on without some of the horses that were shot. . ." Jessie went on and on. Elizabeth closed her eyes again, bored of the tone of Jessie's voice.

Jessie was tall for a woman, probably five-foot-nine. She seemed even taller because she piled her salt and pepper hair on top of her head. She had sharp dark eyes, and crinkles around them from laughing through her forty-five years. Everything about her screamed "no-nonsense." She had a way of putting people in their place if they bothered her. Many were terrified of her wrath. Emma, her younger sister, was the opposite of Jessie in many ways. Her fair hair had just started to turn white, her blue eyes peered out from under pale lashes. She had freckles, but few wrinkles. No one was ever afraid of sweet, quiet, kind Emma. Elizabeth knew Emma was five years younger than Jessie.

Jessie got up and went outside to see if she could help Sam Le-Beau, a short, red-haired man who traveled with them. Elizabeth could hear them moving some of the supplies out of Sam's wagon. He had to lighten his load since he had lost a horse to the gunshots. The sounds of Sally, his tiny, blond, waif of a wife, screaming like a spoiled child because she did not want to give up her possessions was enough to drive anyone to distraction, but Jessie had a constitution of iron. If anyone could help Sally, Jessie could, after all she had helped Elizabeth. Elizabeth drifted off to sleep again.

* * *

Elizabeth awoke several hours later. The wagon moved in its endless trek towards the setting sun. She sat, surprised that she was no longer dizzy. Pulling a threadbare red and white patchwork quilt around her gray calico nightgown, she stuck her head out of the front flap of the wagon.

"Jessie—" Shocked, Elizabeth beheld a man driving her wagon. She flushed the color of crimson. It was Jared Davidson.

She knew little of Jared, except that he wished to gain land in Oklahoma Territory as the rest of them did. Having been trained in the proper ways of a young lady, she felt embarrassed that she had allowed him to carry her to the wagon yesterday after she collapsed. After all, he was a man she knew nothing about, and he had touched her body, something she had been taught was shameful.

"What are you doing here?" She asked at his back. She noticed how his thick light brown hair curled around his shoulders as he turned his green eyes toward her. A few days-worth of stubble grew on his cheeks. From the looks of him, he was so tall, he would tower over her, but then most people did, since she was only five foot two inches. She wiped her head across her forehead, blinking her bright blue eyes, moving her dark curls to one side of her pale face. In all her eighteen years, she had never ached so much. She must have bruised herself all over when she fainted. When Jared tensed to yank on the reigns, the muscles on his arms revealed a lifetime of hard work.

"Sally LeBeau took ill. Jessie asked me to drive so she could take care of Sally. I don't know where your other friend is." After turning to face the horses, he continued, "How are you? You could sit up here with me." His voice was friendly. She did not hear any threat in it, but she hesitated to trust anyone male. Although, the thought of staying under the canvas bored her.

"I'll come shortly." She closed the flap.

Pulling her clothes on, she noticed how her dress strained around her middle. She only had two dresses, both growing increasingly uncomfortable to wear. Regretfully, she thought of the piles of pretty dresses in her home in Virginia. She had fled too quickly to grab anything. None of them would fit anyway. She remembered her tiny waist with a deep sigh.

Jared held out his hand to steady her as she crawled onto the hard pine bench seat.

"You didn't answer my question." He looked at her out of the corner of one of his squinted eyes. The sun glared overhead.

"What question? Oh, I'm much better, thank you." She felt the heat rise to her face just thinking that a man would dare ask about her "condition." However, after yesterday, there was no hiding it. She had been lying to herself that no one knew about her pregnancy but Jessie and Emma anyway. There were no mirrors in their overstuffed wagon, but Elizabeth knew now that everyone in their small group of travelers knew about the child growing inside of her. She figured she was nearly seven months along. She put her hand to her face. Of course, they all knew. But no one spoke of such things, it was not polite.

Jared did not press the matter further. For that, Elizabeth felt gratitude.

Having just heard Jessie call her name, Jared said, "Elizabeth. I can't believe I've never heard your first name before. It's beautiful, and suits you."

"My friends called me Lizzie."

"Would you mind if I called you Elizabeth?" Jared inquired.

"No."

"Then you must call me Jared."

She said nothing.

"I can see you have a problem."

"What are you talking about?" Elizabeth looked up quickly.

He looked at her middle. He did not have to say what he meant.

"I was taught not to discuss such things in mixed company." She felt her face heat.

"Out west no one tries to mask the obvious. Life is too harsh to bother with silly proprieties. But I can see you don't want to talk about it." She remained silent. The Conestoga wagon jerked along, and the afternoon passed.

\* \* \*

For two days Elizabeth had not seen Jared for more than a few minutes. Her eyes swept the horizon. She would not even admit to herself that she missed him. *It's just that he is the only one who seems to care about me besides Jessie and Emma.* Tonight Jeremiah Brown, their wagon train leader, had announced a dance.

Since she felt much better, she almost looked forward to it. *Maybe he will be*—she caught herself before she let herself think that Jared would be there.

The music of a fiddle and a few harmonicas floated through the air three hours later. Jessie and Elizabeth washed their faces with rags soaked with river water warmed over the fire a few feet from the wagon. Elizabeth held her breath so she would not smell the river water. *Ew.*

"Emma, now you got to come with us. You can't stay here all night all by yourself." Jessie grabbed Emma's thin hand. Emma yanked it back.

"I haven't danced since my Homer died. I couldn't, knowing he wouldn't be there to hold me. It's too painful." Emma said.

"Emma, it's been three years, for heaven's sake! Live! The Almighty don't want you sitting around feeling sorry for yourself, and neither would Homer. What would Ma and Pa say?"

"I can't."

"Well, dig your own grave! Come on, Lizzie." Jessie pulled Elizabeth along.

"Emma's got to cheer up a bit. She worries me." Jessie said as their feet crunched the pine needles as they walked toward the sound of the music.

"She will in her own time, Jessie. Stop fretting. Pain just takes time to heal."

"I'm sorry, girl, I forgot you suffer too. You seem to be doing better than she, and your pain is even closer. I think what Emma needs is a good time."

"Good evening, ladies," Doctor LeRoy Kensington Sims tipped his hat to them. "May I escort you to the dance?" In a glance she took in more about Doc than she had before. He was forty-something, tall, brown eyes, dark hair, broad shoulders, with a pudgy middle. Jessie had said Doc spent too much time at gambling tables. She had not seen him since he had examined her following the holdup. Even if he was a doctor, the knowledge that he had examined her caused her face to burn.

"Why I'd be delighted." Jessie took the offered arm and batted her eyes. Elizabeth ignored the other one.

They arrived at the appointed place just as someone began calling a familiar square dance. Elizabeth had danced this all her life. Still, she lingered in the shadows.

"A penny for your thoughts." A deep voice broke her silence.

*Jared Davidson.* The sight of his uncharacteristically clean-shaven face stampeded her heart into her throat. She could tell he had tried to smooth his hair, but it still curled softly around his shoulders. A long-sleeved white shirt tucked into black trousers set off his tanned skin. He wore a leather jacket to protect against the night chill. She smelled strong soap.

Elizabeth swallowed the lump in her throat that she knew was her heart. She said, "I remember when my Papa used to dance this with me when I was just a little girl."

"And I'm sure you have danced this dance with more than your Papa." Jared smiled, his green eyes scorching holes through her blue ones.

She turned away.

"May I?" He held out his hand, palm up, inviting her.

She took it. Confusing thoughts ran through her mind. *Why am I afraid of every man in the world but him?* She had not even shuddered when he touched her. *Why do I trust him? Why does he want to dance with me?* Elizabeth could not understand her feelings. The music changed to a waltz. Jared's eyes questioned hers. When he saw the response he sought, he pulled her close. The comfort she felt next to him vaulted her back to the last time she had felt so safe. At a dance a year ago, she would have been dressed in the finest crinoline petticoats and stiff, shiny ball gown, but had not felt any better than she did now. She pulled her worn coat tighter as Jared's arms moved around hers.

*Papa. Jared reminds me of Papa.* But Papa was dead. And she was all alone. *Or was she?* She wished she could go on feeling this safe forever. The stars twinkled above. She prayed the dance would never end.

# 2

# *The Outlaws*

Beginning to break through the damp darkness, the first warmth of day settled on Elizabeth's face, gently waking her from a deep slumber. She rolled over, and suddenly a sharp pain stabbed her side. *Ouch!* She jumped, but realized only a rough stone lay under her bedroll. *Now how did that get in the wagon?*

She shivered. *We must be crazy to travel like this in the winter.* She dressed and pulled the quilt over her coat in an effort to keep warm.

The now familiar stir of the circled wagons brought a slight comfort. Elizabeth only shuddered to think of what lay behind her, far away in Virginia. She placed a hand on her abdomen. Her child would never know its father. She would make sure of that.

Elizabeth smiled and replied to the morning greetings around her. Jessie and Emma emerged from the small canvas tent they shared. Jessie fed the horses while Emma prepared breakfast. Guilty feelings crept into Elizabeth's mind. The older women constantly urged her to rest, but Elizabeth wanted to do her share. They made her sleep in the tiny space of the wagon so she would be off the ground, and they shared the old tent.

Even in the safety of a group, not many women would dare travel in 1889 without a male escort. Jessie and Emma had persuaded the men traveling in their party that they were more than capable. A grin manifested itself on Elizabeth's face in spite of her painful memories. When Jeremiah Brown, their leader, and Doc Sims, his friend, had tasted Jessie's mouthwatering biscuits they were like soft clay in her hands.

She thought of what had brought them together. They had all fallen victim to the disease some called "land fever." Elizabeth had heard the others explain that a man named David Payne had worked to get Indian Territory lands unassigned to tribes or individuals opened to settlers. Finally, years after Payne had begun his work, the dream would become a reality. As soon as the President of the United States signed the proposed proclamation, there would be free land for the taking as long as you had your Winchester ready to fight claim jumpers. The homesteads called their names from a place everyone now called *Oklahoma*, which meant "Land of the Red Man." They had even heard women could file claims as long as they were single and over twenty-one.

Bending over at the fire, she looked across the circle of six wagons. She jerked when a man's voice spoke to her, "Good morning."

Elizabeth jumped, and looked up, way up. The owner of the voice turned the corners of his mouth up, looking deeply into her eyes. *Jared.* She had never seen such bright green eyes on a tanned face. He wore a shirt that had once been red, and over it a leather vest. Long, but sturdy legs were clad in faded blue work trousers.

"Good morning, Mr. Davidson." Unconsciously, she raised a finger to her mouth to bite a nail. She did not know how to act after their closeness of the previous evening.

He shifted one leg, causing her to notice his worn, but well-greased boots. "Howdy, Mrs. Duncan, are you feeling alright today?"

"I danced last night, didn't I?" Elizabeth looked into his eyes, grinning.

"Um, ahem. Good day. You sure did. I enjoyed myself. I hope you did too." She blushed and looked down and her hands. He tipped his hat, turned on his heel, and walked back to his cattle.

She stared after him, wondering again who he really was. She knew so little about him. He had joined the rest of them outside of Nashville to travel to Oklahoma Territory. Jessie, Emma, Elizabeth, along with two families, and a few single men made up a rag-tag team of vagabonds headed to their promised land. They traveled together because none of them had the funds required to secure train fare for such a long journey.

"Elizabeth, what are you doing awake? I told Emma to let you sleep. You need your rest you know." Jessie sauntered towards her, casually leading Stocking, their black horse with one white foot and Sleeper, the dapple-gray horse.

"I couldn't sleep knowing you had so much to do." Elizabeth pulled herself up, her hands pushing at the pain in her back. Jessie settled down to eat their morning meal of grits and honey as Elizabeth began hitching the horses.

Jessie had been the hired cook in Elizabeth's uncle's Virginia home. When Elizabeth had decided to flee, she had knocked on Jessie's door on the top floor of the mansion. Jessie had borne five sons, and had lost three in infancy. Her youngest son Amos had gone before her to Oklahoma Territory. He waited for the new president's proclamation that would open the promised lands. Amos had written, begging his mother and remaining brother to leave their lives as servants in Elizabeth's uncle's home. Amos would not know until Jessie arrived in Oklahoma Territory that his brother had been left behind in a Virginia churchyard. He had died of scarlet fever. Elizabeth wondered what Amos would think if he could see his mother journeying west without the assistance of her son.

Emma exited the tent. She hitched their second team to the first one. Back in Virginia, Jessie and Elizabeth had used the last of Jessie's hoarded money to purchase tickets to Nashville, where Jessie's sister, Emma, lived. After much coaxing, they had persuaded Emma to join them on their journey. Three years a widow, her children grown, Emma had decided a change might be good for her. Emma had sold her house which gave them the money to buy the Conestoga wagon, horses, and supplies for the journey.

The smaller, more docile, blonde Emma did not chatter as Jessie did. Elizabeth welcomed the quieter companion. She loved Jessie, but her constant chatter did grate on one's nerves once in a while.

Later that same day, as she trudged behind the wagons with a few of their companions, she looked up to see Jared Davidson ride by her. *Now, what was he doing back here?* He usually stayed close to his small herd of cattle. He did not seem to notice her as he galloped his horse to the front of the short train of wagons.

Since life would be unthinkable for a single lady "in the family way," Jessie and Emma had helped Elizabeth construct a story of a husband killed in a duel. She went by *Duncan*, her mother's maiden name instead of her true name, *Lee*, because she wanted no one to find out her true identity. She had no desire for anyone to find out she was unmarried. As an understood widow, even one of eighteen years of age, she could make it in society.

At first, the other women travelers had made an effort to chat with her. She had replied politely, but stiffly, and soon everyone but Jessie and Emma left her alone. Elizabeth thought she would be happier this way, but loneliness engulfed her today. She longed for her best friend Anne Marie with whom she could chatter about anything. But Anne Marie had married last year and moved to Florida. Stooping to fill her ever-present basket with sticks for the mid-day meal fire, she felt the ground shake. Dust in the western sky told her of approaching horses. With relief she saw that it was just a few of their own people. The dust jolted her mind to events four days previous. She shut her blue eyes, grimacing as she remembered the fear the outlaws had caused.

\* \* \*

Dust flying in the air, five filthy, bandana-faced men rode into their camp. Jared Davidson raced alongside her as she darted for cover. His horse foaming, he shouted, "Get in the wagon!"

"Boom!" The shots going off around her, she ran.

All around her people rushed to do the task required: grab guns already loaded in anticipation of this day. Wishing for the safety of a railway car, Elizabeth ran and jumped for the wagon. Her dead father's Winchester lay with her bedroll. She knew little of how to use it, but she grabbed the gun. Gripping it brought some comfort. Jessie was prepared, .38 Colt revolver in hand.

They waited for what seemed like years, lying in the wagon while the shots flew all around them, not knowing who would be dead or alive when they raised their heads. When the beat of the hooves carried the would-be assailants away, the women clambered out of their wagon to assess the damages. The men had persuaded the thieves to ride away after giving them twenty dollars. They had shot a few rounds in the air and terrified a few horses. Four had to be shot because of broken legs.

"Darn Jared Davidson. I wanted to shoot them men dead. He pushed my gun aside and it hit a horse." Walking up to the wagon, Sam LeBeau told Elizabeth as he spit a stream of tobacco.

"I'll be seeing to Sally." Sam said, as he peered into the back of the LeBeau wagon. Sally LeBeau had her two children, one under each arm. Holding them tight, she sobbed. "I hate this land! I want to go back to Nashville. I'm going back. I hate this!" Sally shook with emotion. Elizabeth could hear her outburst.

Elizabeth climbed into the wagon, pulling Sally into her arms. Sally's two-year-old Johnny clung to Elizabeth also. Little seven-year-old Jenny lay on her face sobbing. Elizabeth did not know who needed more comfort, the woman who understood what had happened, or the children who did not. *Would they ever make it to Oklahoma Territory?* She must not voice that fear to Sally.

"Just think of all that land, Sally. You don't want to go back and live on someone else's. Folks say you don't even have to clear the ground in Oklahoma Territory to put a plow to it. You'll have your own cabin. Maybe even a porch to sit in a rocker and dream on a summer's evening." Slowly, Sally stopped shaking.

Deciding Sally would be fine on her own, Elizabeth unwound herself from the sleeping children. Stooping under the worn canvas that had once been white, she placed her hands around the rough wood of the wagon's rear. Dizziness came over her. She gripped the wagon box tighter, attempting to steady herself. Thinking the spell had passed, she threw a foot over the side. Turning, she started to climb down. The dizzy feeling returned, along with waves of nausea. She emptied her stomach. The ground came up to grab her.

*Darkness.*

# 3

# *The Fall*

SINCE ELIZABETH HAD LOST consciousness after the holdup, Jessie filled in the details of Elizabeth's "spell." Elizabeth mused over what Jessie had told her.

\* \* \*

Sam LeBeau saw her fall and scrambled to her side. "Someone help! She's fainted! Get the doc!"

Jared came running, scooping her into his arms. Elizabeth awoke to the feeling of being carried. She struggled in Jared's arms that were like tight bands of steel around her.

"Hey, the doc's not going to hurt you! Hold still." Jared said.

"No, please, I'm fine." Another sharp pain gripped her. She gasped.

"You are not fine. Something is wrong. I can see you are in pain." Shocked by the depth of concern in his eyes, she relaxed.

They had reached her wagon. Jessie and Emma hovered around as Doc Sims instructed Jared to place Elizabeth on Jessie's pallet of patchwork quilts.

"All right, now everyone skedaddle so I can breathe in here!" Doc Sims barked.

As Jared, Jessie, and Emma clambered out of the wagon, the doctor began to examine Elizabeth. She tried to resist him due to her modesty, but eventually the familiar blackness claimed her.

She heard Jessie cry, "Emma, she's awake!" Her first view took in Jessie wringing the cloth she had been using to keep Elizabeth's forehead cool.

"Praise Jesus." Emma hovered over Elizabeth like a mother hen with a fresh brood of chicks.

"Did they? Did he? Am I?"

"You just stay still. No one's going to send you back home. The Doc said you need rest. Everything's fine." Jessie comforted. Over Elizabeth's head Emma frowned.

Elizabeth felt for her belly. "Is the baby. . ."

"The baby seems just fine." Emma comforted. Elizabeth groaned. Emma heard a sound outside the wagon and jumped, shaking the wagon.

"Mrs. Shows, Mrs. Linn," Someone whispered. Elizabeth could not hear words, only noise.

Jessie stuck her head outside. Jared Davidson, broad-brimmed russet Stetson in hand, asked, "How is she?"

"She's awakened once, but is heading towards sleep again. Doc gave her something."

"Glad to hear it. Wouldn't want to lose a day." Jared replied.

Jessie's hackles rose. "Is that all you menfolk ever think of? There's a very sick young lady in this wagon, and all you can think of is losing a day?" Jessie's voice grew louder.

Elizabeth asked, "Jessie, who is it?"

"It's Mr. Davidson asking after your well-being," Jessie replied.

"Please tell him I will be fine and fit for travel tomorrow." Elizabeth said.

"I'll inform Mr. Brown." Jared turned to go.

"You'll do no such thing. Where is that doctor? I'm fixin' to tell him a thing or two. Did he say she could travel? How can she bear it in a shaking wagon all day?"

\* \* \*

The last thing Elizabeth remembered was Jessie jumping out of the wagon and going in search of the doctor, still muttering threats. Elizabeth lay awake later that night. The sounds of Sally LeBeau's two-year-old fussing drifted through the canvas. After seeing spots of blood on her bedding, she wondered if she would lose this baby. Right now, she did not care what happened. Babies should be conceived in wedlock, and be born into a family complete with two loving parents. Even in her eighteen-year-old innocence she had known that—why had she allowed William to—wait, *what was that*?

A movement, as soft as a butterfly's wing fluttered in her abdomen. It was not the pain she had felt earlier. It was not pain at all. *It must be, it must be. . .*

"Emma! Jessie!" She called.

"Yes, I'm here," Emma poked her head in the back flap of the wagon.

"She's moving. I can feel it moving again! That means it's ok!"

"Praise Jesus!" Emma exclaimed.

"The baby is moving." Elizabeth sighed and rolled over. She tried to pray. The baby suddenly became a real human being to her, a child under her protection. *God, please let the baby live.* This child would be born. She would be born in a new land, far away.

Dreams fluttered through her mind the entire night. Yet when she woke, only one dream came across her mind. She had been talking with her childhood friend, Anne Marie in the dream.

*"His eyes, Annie, they looked right through me."* Elizabeth *giggled. In this dream, they were both fifteen, and sitting on the front porch of her uncle's southern mansion. Elizabeth could smell the roses as she sat with Anne Marie.*

*"You always say that, Lizzie, I keep telling you there's much more to choosing a man than liking his eyes."*

*"You sound like my aunt. You've only just been engaged yourself, even if you are fifteen." Elizabeth said to Anne Marie.*

Running over the dream in her mind, Elizabeth once again dragged herself out of the wagon. His eyes. She had never had this conversation with Anne Marie, had she? Thoughts of Jared's eyes seeing through to her soul made her connect the dream to him. What was she doing? How had she let him dance with her that entire evening? She could never, never let anyone close to her again. *Why? Why did I allow him to get so close?*

The sound of Jessie singing brought her to reality. "You're in a good mood this morning," Elizabeth said as Jessie stirred pancakes and prepared to pour them in a cast iron skillet on the fire.

"Yes, it's a beautiful day." Jessie smiled.

"Jessie, it's cloudy and it looks like rain. What's wrong with you?"

"Nothing."

Emma joined them.

"You sure missed a good time at the dance the other night." Jessie teased.

"I spent the time praying, thinking about my Homer." Emma frowned.

"Please, Emma, it's about time you lived."

"I don't want to discuss it." Emma stomped away from their camp, her small boots making indentions in the dark soft dirt.

"I hope it doesn't rain. This excuse for ground we're trekking across will become nothing but deep, dark mud." Elizabeth tried to change the subject.

Jessie obviously had not heard her. Her eyes scanned the camp. "Looking for someone?" Elizabeth asked.

"No, just seeing who's up and around." Jessie went back to cooking.

"Mrs. Shows—please—come—quick, it's my Sally!" A breathless Sam LeBeau yelled.

"He must be in the wagon," Jessie ran, Elizabeth on her heels.

They could hear screaming. Opening the wagon flap, Elizabeth peered in to find Sally holding Sam's Winchester rifle. The barrel of the gun was shoved against Sam's chest.

"I ain't going no further! We're going back home and no one will stop us! I never wanted to come on this trip! You made me! I hate you!" Sally's shrieks filled the air like the sounds of a crow in distress. Sam began pleading with his wife to calm down.

"Sally, please put the gun down. What if you hurt the children?" Sam said.

"Shut up!" Sally shrieked, yanking the gun away, pointing it upward. Sam reached for it. Sally fought him. While Sally was distracted, Jessie ran around to the front of the wagon and pulled Johnny and Jenny out the back flap. Elizabeth ran to help her.

"BOOM!"

# 4

# *Sally*

THE GUN SHOT A hole through the canvas and brought screams across the camp. Jeremiah and Jared came running in a flash of boots, jeans, Stetsons, and dust.

"What do you think you're doing, LeBeau?" Jeremiah's voice contained a sharpness the camp had never heard.

"It weren't me, it was Sally." Sally had fallen over and was now shaking uncontrollably.

"Slap her!" Jared ordered as he looked over the wagon at the hysterical woman.

Sam obeyed. Sally calmed. She went limp and only an occasional hiccup came out of her mouth as she drooled.

Elizabeth climbed into the wagon. She pulled Sally into her arms and held her. "Shh. Shh. Everything's going to be alright." She comforted. She could hear the men talking outside. Jessie gathered the children, and moved to take them to her own wagon. Johnny's voice broke her heart,

"I-I w-want M-ma."

"We're leaving you at the next town," Jeremiah told Sam.

"You can't. I don't got nothin.' I need to file a claim in Oklahoma Territory so I can scratch a living! Sally'll straighten up. She ain't done nothing like that before." Sam's voice shook. Holding Sally, Elizabeth felt sorry for him.

"Is Mama sick?" Elizabeth heard Jenny ask Jessie.

"Yeah darling, she needs her rest. We best go so she can sleep. Come on, children." The voices melted into the morning sunlight as Jessie led them away to her tent. Elizabeth was sure Jessie and Emma would wrap them in their own soft quilts for the night.

Later that day as Elizabeth sloshed soiled garments in a muddy creek, Mildred, a short, brown-haired, blue-eyed woman, came to talk to her. Elizabeth welcomed the company. She tried to be friendly, hoping the woman would forget how cold she had been towards her. Although inclined to let her tongue wag, Mildred Johnson seemed to be a sweet woman.

"I hear Mr. Brown's leaving the LeBeaus at the next town," Mildred commented.

"That's what I heard." Elizabeth wondered how anything could come clean in this murky water. She rubbed a knitted green wool sock on the rough washboard. How she hated washing clothes, something she had never done until this journey.

"It's a shame. My George says that some ladies that just ain't cut out for the living beyond the comforts of the East."

"Guess so." Elizabeth determined she *would* be cut out for this rugged life. *No one will ever say those words about me, even if I give birth in a moving wagon.*

"Who did I see you dancing with the other night?" Mildred changed the subject. She picked up a clean garment and hung it on Elizabeth's makeshift clothesline, strung between two poplars.

"I danced with all the men." Annoyance tinged her voice despite her efforts to remain pleasant.

"No, I saw you with someone that seemed special."

"No man is special to me."

"Yes, it was that good looking fellow, Mr. Davidson, I believe."

"Yes, I danced with him."

"You blushed in his arms."

"How could you see that in the firelight, Mildred?" Elizabeth was beginning to wish she had not welcomed Mildred's company.

She splashed in the murky frigid water. Her chapped, raw hands were freezing in the biting wind.

Just then Mildred's son Jacob ran to her.

"Mama, come quick, it's Becky. She won't quit crying."

"My daughter," she said to Elizabeth, turning to run after Jacob.

Elizabeth felt relief flood through her like the wash water flowing on the ground when it overflowed the tub. She was sure she had turned the color of a tomato at the mention of Jared's name. She hated herself for it. Maybe Mildred would not bring it up again.

Walking toward camp that evening, Elizabeth noticed three people silhouetted against the night sky around her fire. As she approached, Doc Sims stood in greeting. "Howdy," he said, as he stood to his feet and removed his black Stetson, revealing his thick head of gray wavy hair.

"Hello, Doctor," Elizabeth lowered her growing body to the ground, easing her weary back against a wagon wheel.

"I asked the Doc to join us for supper," Jessie explained.

Elizabeth squirmed. She did not like eating with the man who had seen her undressed. She ate quietly, as did Emma. Jessie and the doctor kept a running conversation about politics.

"Ol' Harrison, if he knows what's good for him will allow this land to be opened soon. I read in *Harper's* just before I left that the towns along the border of the unassigned lands are busting with people waiting to get their own land."

"Just hope he waits until we get there!" Jessie said.

"I may be a doctor, but I want 160 acres to call my own just as other men want. Then I'll set up a practice in a nearby town. I hear that Guthrie is the place to go. That's where one of the land offices is. I heard predictions that'll be the biggest settlement in the territory."

For the first time since they had begun the journey, Elizabeth wondered why a doctor could not afford train fare. She knew it would be impolite to inquire into the matter, so she tried to squelch her curiosity.

"Sure seems a shame for all those Indians to lose their land." Emma suddenly joined the conversation.

Elizabeth looked at quiet little Emma, clad in a red calico dress, shocked. She had never heard anyone give sympathy to the Indians concerning this matter.

"Paid them fair and square. Four million bucks fair and square," Doc said, "Besides, them savage Indians don't need this good land. They don't farm it."

"How do you know? They've been driven out of their own lands for years into Indian Territory. Now the government is taking even that away."

"Humph." The doctor snorted. The conversation ended. But for the first time, Elizabeth questioned what they were doing. Maybe it was not the right thing to take away the Indians' land.

The next day they passed through Memphis, Tennessee, a bustling city. Jeremiah Brown was heard arguing with Sam LeBeau about leaving Sam's family behind. Their voices got louder and louder, but finally, Sam convinced Jeremiah that he would make sure Sally calmed.

At the western edge of the city, Jessie gave Elizabeth a few coins and told her to go buy dinner. It was just a short walk to the general store. It had been so long since she had seen "civilization," the amount of goods took her by surprise. Behind the counter, bolts of brightly colored calico filled the shelves. A huge barrel of pickles stood next to the counter, the sharp smell rising to her nostrils. *How good it would feel to sink her teeth in. . .*

"Ma'am, may I help you?" The storekeeper interrupted her thoughts. She handed him the list Jessie had made. As he filled the order, she dreamed of the pretty dresses she could make with the pink and purple calico.

Using the ingredients from the store, Elizabeth prepared a meal of vegetable stew. Jessie had been instructing her in the fine art of cooking over an open fire. Elizabeth chuckled to herself as if she had known how to cook on a stove. She had never cooked a meal until this trip. She struggled to cut the carrots and onions with a dull knife as she knelt on the ground next to a battered blue tin plate. Water in the heavy black cast iron pot took forever to boil. A few pieces of dried beef made a broth and she poured in some salt and pepper.

The smell haunted the camp. Jessie and Emma praised her culinary efforts. They were camped on the edge of the great Mississippi, the gateway to the West. In the distance they heard the water lap at the edge of the shore. Tomorrow they would cross on a ferry. Elizabeth tried not to think about the journey over the water on a rickety boat.

"You're going to catch a man yet, Elizabeth." Jessie joked.

"Excuse me, please." Elizabeth pushed herself up off the rocky ground. She still could not talk about men or romance. As she walked away, she heard Emma and Jessie remarking on the newspaper they had bought in Memphis. "Harrison hasn't opened the lands, yet, thankfully."

"Wait, Lizzie!" Jessie yelled but Elizabeth kept walking. She made her way over to the LeBeau's wagon.

"Good evening, Sally," she called as she approached their fire. Sally made no reply. She simply sat, hugging her knees humming a tuneless melody. Sam looked up from the attempt he had made at cooking supper.

"Here, let me help." She scooped helpings of the stew into tin plates for Jenny and Johnny.

Sally got up and walked into the twilight. Sam looked at Elizabeth.

"I don't know what to do. She won't talk. She just sits and rocks herself like that. She don't tend the children. Mr. Brown says he's dropping us at the next town. For what? Everything I own is in this wagon. I need that land in Oklahoma Territory!" Sam's voice broke as he wiped his brow.

"I can help, Pa," Jenny chimed.

"I know. You're a big help, Jenny. Why don't you help Johnny get ready for bed?" Jenny pulled Johnny to her.

"She's growing up too fast. She should be playing like other seven-year-olds; instead she's chasing her little brother like an old schoolmarm." Sam began to scrape plates.

Elizabeth washed the dishes for him in a dishpan full of river water. She walked back to her own camp only after she had settled Johnny and Jenny in their wagon. Emma, her small form wrapped in a red and white checkerboard quilt, sat next to the fire by herself, knitting. She told Elizabeth that the Doctor and Jessie had gone to check on Mildred's Becky who had hurt her ankle earlier.

An hour later, shouts awoke Elizabeth. Scrambling to her feet, she wrapped her yellow and blue quilt around her flannel nightgown and peeked out the canvas hole.

"What's going on?" Emma asked, rubbing her sleep-filled eyes.

"I don't know; I'm going to see." Jessie emerged from her tent, throwing her black coat around her as she ran. Emma was fast on her heels, barefoot. Elizabeth climbed to the ground, carefully.

"She can't be far." She heard Jared's voice. She ran towards the voice, stumbling in the darkness as fast as her pregnant body would safely take her.

"What's the matter? Who can't be far?" She screamed at him as the men of the camp raced around her, torches lit from campfires in their hands.

"Sally. She never came back from her walk. We told her and told her not to walk away from the wagons. Hey, you just go back to sleep. We'll take care of it." Jared ran to get his horse, as he ran, he yelled back, "Someone ride back to Memphis and see if there's a sheriff hereabouts."

Mildred's husband, George, hollered that he would do it.

Elizabeth stopped to light a torch as she tried to make her way to the LeBeau wagon. Jenny had her arms around Johnny, barely visible in the darkness. The children's anguished cries filled the night air.

"Where's Ma?" Jenny wailed. Johnny's cries joined hers.

"They'll find her, now don't you worry." Emma sat on the ground holding both children.

"Where's Jessie?" Elizabeth asked as she sank to the cold hard ground and took Johnny in her arms.

"She's out looking with the men." Elizabeth rubbed Johnny's shaking little back as he put his blond curls on her shoulder. Elizabeth tried not to think of all the things that could go wrong. She tried not to think of the raging river less than a hundred feet from their camp. Emma began to pray aloud.

Elizabeth breathed a prayer herself. She never prayed much, outside of church, but now she did not know what else to do. Suddenly the thought crossed her mind that maybe God would not hear a prayer from someone like her. *Oh no.* She had never thought of that before. *Well, I can try, can't I?* She shot a few desperate sentences up past the stars, hoping the Father above would find them.

Elizabeth's head jerked. She must have fallen asleep. She and Emma had drawn Johnny and Jenny into their father's tent and settled them. *What had awakened her?* Then she heard male voices. Jared's face was at the opening tent canvas. In the murky first light of day, her eyes questioned his. He shook his head. She crawled towards the tent door and the children awakened around her. Emma sat up and they all exited the tent, standing to their feet. Elizabeth shivered even though she was fully clothed in her coat and shoes.

Elizabeth saw Sam LeBeau walking towards her in the morning haze. He held a woman in his arms. Sally. When he got closer, she knew. Sally was dead. Elizabeth choked back a sob.

"Ma!" Jenny had jumped from the wagon.

"Ma!" She screamed. Elizabeth pulled her close. They sobbed together. Jessie wrapped her arms around both of them.

A few hours later, the same broken-hearted men that had found Sally face down, floating on the edge of the river, lowered Sally's body into the ground. Jessie had wrapped the still form in a worn blanket. *Not even a coffin*, thought Elizabeth. She shuddered, thinking it could have been her in that cold ground. She placed her hand on her small mound of belly. *What if it were her baby left without a mother?* Jeremiah Brown said a few words over the grave.

Jeremiah had called a day of rest due to the funeral. They could put off crossing the Mississippi another day. Elizabeth spent it with the LeBeau children. She and Jessie took turns sitting around the fire, telling the little ones stories to occupy their sorrowful minds.

"Mama!" Johnny's voice wailed. Elizabeth wiped his face on her coat sleeve. No one could comfort him. The weather had turned from mild to cold. The children sniffled and hiccupped as they huddled close to the fire, wrapped in Jessie's red and white checkerboard quilt. *What I wouldn't give for a roof over my head and a hot wood stove,* thought Elizabeth.

Sam simply sat staring into the fire. Jessie had tried to get him to eat to no avail. Mildred had been by to offer some hot food. She had not stayed since she had her own family to tend. No one knew what to say.

Jessie came by, so Elizabeth decided to return to her own wagon. *Maybe if I curl up in more quilts, I'll get warm.* A sudden burst of rain shocked her into realizing the world still worked as it had yesterday. The drops soaked through her wool coat and her thin dress, making her teeth chatter.

"How's the young'uns?" She heard Jared's voice. Her heart jumped.

"Crying. That's what they need to do." Elizabeth's voice shook. Jared turned to her.

"And how are you?" His eyes showed deep concern.

"I'm fine. I didn't just lose my mother." Elizabeth replied. Yet all the mourning of Jenny and Johnny reminded her of the day her uncle had told her of her parents' death. She had been only eight, and her parents had both died of diphtheria. Her world had crumbled around her.

"Mrs. Duncan, there are other kinds of sorrow."

"Mr. Davidson, I believe I'm well aware of that."

The rain poured around them. They were shouting to be heard. She continued to shiver with cold. He took his coat off and wrapped it around her. A sob escaped her throat like an animal in pain. He pulled her close. She did not know how long they stood there in the rain. She did not know how long she cried. Her tears mingled with the raindrops and once again she imagined her father held her. She was safe. Though they were both soaked to the skin, Jared's arms sheltered her from the storm raging inside.

*Part Two*

# *Arkansas*

March, 1889

# 5

# *Unforgiveness*

A WEEK PASSED, IN which Elizabeth spent as much time with the LeBeau little ones as possible. They stayed with her during the day, she and Jessie taking turns carrying little Johnny or holding him on the wagon. Jenny seemed only to want Emma. Jenny attached herself to the older woman, trying to find comfort in a world that had fallen apart. Emma's arms, long empty of her own babies, welcomed the little tyke.

A few days later, Elizabeth sat under a bare blackjack tree somewhere in Arkansas. She leaned against the strong trunk and shut her eyes.

"Sleeping during the day?" A voice teased.

She opened her eyes to see Jared, his green eyes bright.

"Hello."

"Mind if I join you?"

"No, just don't expect me to say much. I'm beat."

"Funny, but I get the impression that this kind of life is agreeing with you."

"What do you mean, Mr. Davidson?" Elizabeth bit at a hangnail.

"Well, you seem to fit right in the roughness, I guess."

"Is that a compliment?" The wind shifted. She shivered.

"Yep."

"Well, thank you, then. I'm not used to living outside, much less traveling in the winter like this." She pulled her wool coat around her, and tied her hat strings tighter. Jared sat down next to her, exhaling as he bent.

"Spring weather could hit any time. You must be from somewhere further east than Nashville."

"It was my understanding that Westerners did not inquire about the pasts of people." Her voice sounded sharp. She cringed, thinking she must have been rude.

"Sorry. I was just making conversation." He unwound his legs and moved to stand up and leave.

"No, no, Mr. Davidson, I'm sorry. I spoke too sharply. You must forgive me." She patted the ground next to her so he would know she was serious.

"Sure."

"I'm from Virginia." There. She had said it for the first time since fleeing the state.

"Oh."

"And you?"

"Kansas."

"I've never known anyone born that far west."

"My parents settled there right before I was born."

"Move out!" Jeremiah's voice boomed across the camp.

"Later." In one smooth movement, Jared sprung to his feet and raced to his wagon. Elizabeth wondered if she would ever be that light on her feet again. She carefully maneuvered her feet under her belly, using the tree trunk to steady herself. She pulled herself up, all the while noting Jared's tender care of his ten head of cattle. *He loves those animals. I wonder why. He takes care of them like they are his children.*

Last night Jeremiah had announced they were nearing the final stages of the journey. In a few days they would reach Fort Smith. Indian Territory loomed in front of them. Elizabeth tried not to let her anxiety take over all of her thoughts, but for a moment gave into the pressure of the fleeting fears. For so long the only thought on her mind had been getting away from Virginia, and away from William, Uncle Jacob, and Aunt Jane. Now the apprehensive contemplation concerning her future began to override the concerns of the past.

As she mindlessly prepared once again for a monotonous day moving from uncomfortable wagon seat to trudging behind the wagons, she worriedly chewed her nails. Anne Marie, her girlhood friend, had always teased her about the nail biting. Anne Marie had said, "I always know nervous you have been by the length of your nails."

Today her fingertips bled. She should keep her hands in gloves, but periodically, she pulled her cold hand out of the glove and gnawed on already bitten skin. What if an Indian attacked them like the thieves had done earlier? She must ask someone to teach her to shoot.

"Make way!" She turned to see Jared and another man riding through the group of walking women. Jessie hollered beside her.

"Mr. Davidson, come to supper with us tonight!"

"Be obliged!" He returned and was soon out of sight.

"Why did you do that?" asked Elizabeth as she shifted Johnny to her other hip.

"Here, give him to me, you shouldn't be carrying him anyway." Jessie looked down at Elizabeth's expanding stomach.

Johnny whined, "I hungry, Miss Jessie."

"It's almost dinner time, child, hush." Jessie reassured him, patting his back as his blond curls bounced with her gait.

"I'm glad Jeremiah didn't leave Sam behind at the last town." Elizabeth changed the subject.

"Me too. I guess he figured Sally ain't around to make any more trouble, God rest her soul."

Just then Emma caught up with them, Jenny close behind her. Elizabeth had never seen Emma look so young. Emma laughed as Jenny said, "Miss Emma you can't catch me!" Jenny ran. Emma ran, her blond hair falling from its pins and her body a flash of red calico and white apron.

Later that evening, sitting around the fire, Elizabeth looked across to see Jared staring at her. She blushed, looking down at her ugly gnawed nails. Emma had gone over to put the children to bed. Jessie suddenly arose, "Well, I'll be turning in. Just leave these dishes to wash with the breakfast ones, Elizabeth." She disappeared into her tent.

Jared moved closer. Elizabeth began to squirm.

Jared explained, and then asked, "How do you plan to support yourself once you get to Oklahoma Territory?"

"I haven't thought about it. I was too busy just trying to get away from Virginia, and then too busy trying to survive this endless journey. I just don't know." Elizabeth's voice shook. "Are all western men like you, minding their own business?" A hint of sarcasm tinged her voice, but the corners of her mouth tried to turn up to let him know she was teasing.

"Out west you don't judge anyone on their past. No one asks. If you measure up, it's because you're you and you do your job well. A lot of folks don't use their own names, but no one questions. It was rude of me to question you earlier today."

Elizabeth jumped. He would never know she did not use her own name. He would not ask. She would not tell him.

"Then I suppose it wouldn't be polite for me to ask you to tell me about yourself."

"No, but you're from the East, you don't know any better, so I'll tell you something. There's not much to tell, but I really don't have much to hide. I watched my ma and pa die by the hands of Indians. I hid in a cupboard when they raided our house. I never met an Indian I like."

Elizabeth had not expected him to reveal so much about himself. She was taken aback by his brutal honesty, and a little scared of his hatred. She had never liked Indians, but she did not feel this intense hatred for them either.

"I can see you were hurt deeply. I'm so sorry about your parents. Can't you forgive and go on?" She offered him what she had heard in church.

"Forgive? You didn't see what I saw. I will never forgive."

"But, Jared, God says he won't forgive us if we don't forgive others." Elizabeth stunned herself. *What had she just said? God won't forgive. No way in a thousand lifetimes would she ever forgive William for what he did to her. If God wouldn't forgive her, she would have to deal with hellfire.*

"God must not think much of me to have allowed a tragedy to happen to me so young. What about you? You're a widow. Don't you question him for taking away your husband?" Jared's green eyes were suddenly cold.

Elizabeth turned her head. If only he knew the truth. But instead of addressing the subject, she tried to stand. He jumped to his feet quickly and pulled her up. She wanted to resist, but how could she? Her back hurt, her feet ached, and her face froze.

"Excuse me, Jared; I believe it's time to say good night." With that, she turned and climbed into the wagon, loosed the strings on her corset, and wormed her way into her bedroll without undressing or even taking off her shoes. She shivered. Through the hole in the canvas, she saw him douse the fire and trudge towards his own wagon.

# 6

# *The Proposal*

NEARLY HALFWAY ACROSS ARKANSAS, near the town of Conway, Elizabeth, wedged between wagon side and flour sack, caught a sob in her throat. She swallowed the lump, not wanting to wake the other two. *Oh William, why? Why did you do it?* The child inside kicked. Hard. Then the baby wedged a foot under her rib. The dull ache spread through her body. She could no longer distinguish the physical aching from the emotional. William's child. *No, I can't think of it that way. I cannot hold William's sin against this baby. I cannot scar her that way. She will never know the anguish that I have known.*

*Drat that Jared. He made me think about it again. He made me start to question.* She had never thought to blame God for her pain. She, of course, thought God was simply punishing her for her sins. She had always felt she deserved it. Now she started questioning. *What about those who sin as I did and do not get punished this way? Why? Why don't you punish them too God? Why did you punish me? Drat Jared!* She would have to avoid talking to him if this was the outcome. She would rather just not think at all about the past or the future, but even as she allowed herself to feel as if she did not want to think or dread, the thoughts crashed through her mind like a storm across the distant hills.

*The Bible says to take one day at a time, that's what I'm trying to do.* Finally, her thoughts abated, weariness won, and she succumbed to the waves of slumber.

Next morning as she scrubbed the breakfast dishes, she noticed Sam creeping up to her fire. Pain still etched across his face. Her heart went out to him.

"Good morning, Sam, how are the children?" Elizabeth asked.

"Fine." He held twirled his hat in his hands, his red hair stood on end, and he looked at his feet, seemingly wishing the earth would open and swallow him.

"Tell Jenny I'll be over to see them as soon as I finish morning chores." Elizabeth started to climb in the wagon where Emma was packing the tent away for the day.

"Wait, uh, Mrs. Duncan, I-I n-need to talk to you." The urgency in his voice made her stop, turn around, and climb down, yet with difficulty

"Yes, Sam, what is it?"

"Well, I need to talk to you private-like." Sam did look as if he wished the earth would open up and swallow him. Jessie, who had been squatting next to the fire drinking her coffee, took the hint, and sauntered away towards Mildred's wagon. She looked back once, like a child excused from the supper table before her favorite dessert.

Elizabeth moved toward Sam. "Yes, Sam, what's on your mind? Is it about Johnny? Look, I know he's been fussy, but if you just let me. . .."

"No, it's not Johnny, It's me, well, it's us. . ..well, I uh, that is, we uh, well, I uh."

"Sam, what's wrong, you can tell me, whatever it is, I'll listen."

"I uh will you marry me?"

Elizabeth froze. She dropped the shawl in her hand. The words sunk in like the cold March wind, biting the pain of a past proposal's memories. All the polite responses she had been taught as a girl slipped her mind and instead, she blurted, "Sam, no, I can't."

"Wait, let me explain. I know you must think I'm terribly forward, not knowing you long, but listen to me. I've got two young'uns without a mama, and I know you uh well uh." His nervous eyes glanced at her growing middle. "You uh need uh help with uh you know."

"No, Sam."

Now that he had started talking, he couldn't seem to stop. He argued, "But it's just a trade I'm thinking on. You watch after my young'uns and I'll be providing for you and yours. I done a lot of thinking before I said this. . .."

"Sam, I don't know what to say. . . I respect you, but I don't love you. How can I marry you?"

"Love? In case you haven't noticed no one gets married for love in the west! We need each other, and I well, I uh, won't be asking you to be doing any wifely duties." He blushed, twirling his hat again, looking down at his worn black pointed-toe boots. Not just his face, but all of his skin that showed blazed red.

"I just don't think so, Sam."

"Will you think on it? Will you at least promise me that?" Sam's brown eyes pleaded.

"I'll. . .."

"Sam, I'll marry you." Elizabeth jumped as she heard another woman's voice. She turned around. It was Emma. She had overheard the conversation from the wagon. Now she leaped down and stood squarely in front of Sam.

"Did you hear me, Sam? I said I'd marry you."

* * *

"Now, Jessie, explain this to me again, who is marrying whom?" Mildred trudged beside Jessie just far enough behind the wagons to avoid the ever-present dust.

"I done told you. Emma said she's going to be marrying up with Sam LeBeau! This Sunday! Can you believe it? I thought Emma was out of her mind, but I didn't know it was this bad." Jessie shook her head and spat a stream of tobacco at a large boulder.

"Well, Jessie, Sam does need a wife to tend to those young'uns, you know. I can't blame him for asking a capable woman like Emma even if she is older than him." Mildred said.

"That's just it, he didn't ask her. He asked Eliz. . ." Jessie stopped short as she saw Elizabeth catch up to them.

"Morning, Elizabeth." Mildred and Jessie said in unison.

"Morning." Elizabeth's breath was labored.

"You should be in the wagon, girl," Mildred prodded her.

"I can't stand to stay under that canvas, nor sit on the seat in front." The real reason she would not stay had nothing to do with that. Today was Emma's turn to drive and she could not bear to be near Emma at the moment.

"Pray tell what you think about Sam and Emma, Elizabeth?" Mildred looked at Elizabeth expectantly.

"I imagine they'll make it work. They're both responsible. Excuse me." Elizabeth stopped to pick up some sticks for the fire so they would not look at her. She prayed they would move on and leave her alone. No such luck. When she stood, they were waiting for her.

"I know it's not the best circumstances, but weddings always bring out the romancing in me." Mildred sighed dramatically.

"Humph," said Jessie, "Romancing usually lasts all of one day, then it is life as usual."

"You're too practical, Jessie." Mildred said.

"Excuse me, I think I see little Johnny giving Jenny a hard time, I think I'll go help." Elizabeth hurried away.

"What were you saying before she walked up, Jessie?"

"I was telling you Sam didn't ask Emma. He asked Elizabeth to marry him." Jessie said.

"No wonder she was so fidgety, but how in the world did Emma end up. . .?"

"She overheard Elizabeth turning him down and walked up saying she would marry him," said Jessie, "I can't believe it. Emma is so quiet and proper-like. Here she is practically throwing herself at a man."

"Well it ain't as if I ain't seen you do the same thing with the Doc."

Jessie aimed another stream of tobacco at a rut in the road. She took a fresh plug out of the shiny tin in her coat pocket.

"I ain't proposing to him."

Up ahead they saw the wagons stopping for the noon meal. They chatted amiably until they parted at their separate camps in order to prepare the food.

\* \* \*

When Elizabeth left them with her lame excuse, she tried to figure out why this marriage was bothering her so much. It was not as if she had wanted to marry Sam. After all, this was not the first time someone had proposed to her. Or even the second. Then. . . there was that time. . . she drifted away in a remembrance of times past.

*They had stood beneath the white gazebo in her parents' garden. The lilacs bloomed bright and purple, filling the air with their scent. In addition, the fragrance of roses floated through the spring air. William, tall, dark eyes shining, and straight brown hair slicked back stood above her smiling. He had led her to sit in the gazebo, her pink dress swishing, and the next thing she knew he was down on one knee, with a huge diamond ring, pledging his undying love. She had smiled, batted her eyes, and accepted his offer as a proper young lady should, blushing with happiness. Oh, how the world had seemed beautiful and promising then! Not dark, shadowy, and confusing as it did now.*

She knew what Sam had asked her had not been so unusual. She probably should have told him yes. *How was she going to take care of herself and her baby?* She had heard that women could file a claim in Oklahoma, but she was three years short of the age requirement. Even if she did, how would she work it? Yet something inside her was still too deeply hurt to imagine marrying anyone. She would figure out some way to support this child. She placed her hand on her swollen abdomen. She was rewarded with a sharp kick.

"See, baby, I know you trust your mama. I just hope I can live up to that trust."

The people of the train rejoiced over the idea of a wedding. They cooked and planned and talked and talked until Elizabeth was sure Emma felt like a young woman again. They were more careful to be solemn around Sam, as they knew he was still lost in the sorrow of losing Sally. Yet even Sam could be found hiding a shy grin behind a hoarse cough every now and then.

Sunday morning dawned beautiful and clear. The sun shone, and temperature raised itself enough that Emma would not have to wear a coat over her dress. Emma fussed in the wagon.

"Now, Emma, you just let me take care of it." Jessie ordered.

Elizabeth laughed from where she stirred the morning porridge. She would miss Emma and Jessie fussing at each other.

Emma emerged looking radiant in a gray cashmere dress Elizabeth had never seen.

"I've been saving it for a special occasion." Emma said at her questioning gaze. Her blonde hair was pinned in neat braids around her head.

"Oh, Emma, you look wonderful." Elizabeth hugged her. Jessie came crashing down.

"Girls, we still got chores to do." Jessie took the horses down for their morning watering, hooves clopping on the beaten path to a spring.

"Elizabeth, I've been meaning to talk to you. I hope you're not ashamed at what I'm about to do." Emma's soft brown eyes reached out to Elizabeth as did her small hand, resting on Elizabeth's shoulder.

"Of course, not Emma, please don't fret. But why. . ."

"You're wondering why I said I would do this, aren't you?"

"Yes, I know you still love your Homer, so how can you marry someone you don't love?"

"I'm not strong like you and Jessie, Elizabeth. I've never lived without a man's protection and caring until Homer died a year ago.

I just can't see myself living on my own. Besides, those children need a mama. My babies are all grown now, and I miss tending to them. I know it seems unbecoming to you, but please try to understand. Please." Elizabeth had never heard Emma make such a long speech.

"I understand," said Elizabeth. Even though she did not. What else could she say? Emma's friendship meant more to her than honesty at the moment.

Jessie returned. They ate in relative silence, each lost in her own world of swirling thoughts. *I did not know I was strong,* thought Elizabeth. *As a matter of fact, I feel pretty weak. Why did she call me strong?*

\* \* \*

Elizabeth sat on a rough wool horse blanket, waiting for the wedding ceremony to begin.

"Elizabeth." She jumped. Even though they had told either other their first names, Jared rarely used hers. Although it was impossible to avoid him, she had not talked to him since that fateful night when she had rushed away after hearing his life story. She did not know what to say now.

"May I sit with you?"

"Certainly." She made room for him on the blanket. She wondered what could be keeping Jessie. She could always be counted on for conversation.

"Kind of hard to believe, ain't it? Sam and Emma?" Jared said.

"Yes."

"I hear Sam asked you first. Wonder how Emma feels about being second fiddle?"

"Mr. Davidson, please."

"You don't want to talk about it."

"You guessed it." Elizabeth stiffened her back and looked down at her nails.

"I suppose you're the kind of woman who wouldn't marry someone for convenience."

"Is that supposed to be a compliment?"

"Take it as you want to." He laughed. "Oh, I'm sorry, I forgot. You have been married. Forgive my blundering." He was serious.

"Really, I don't mind. But what kind of a woman do you think I am?"

"Well, you're a romantic. You'd only marry for love and love alone. Even if you do have a young'un to care for," Jared looked her in the eye, his green eyes serious.

"How do you know?"

"I've seen the way you stop and look at a sunset, or a flower. Sometimes you get a dreamy look when you stop to think. I've heard pain in your voice. Someone hurt you. Maybe it was the death of your husband." Jared's voice stopped as Jessie approached.

Jessie sat down just as Doc Sims began the wedding service, his voice booming. His boots shone and his suit, freshly brushed looked nearly new. *Is there anything that man isn't qualified to do?* Elizabeth wondered.

Elizabeth lost in thoughts of Jared's eyes looking deeply into hers did not hear any of the ceremony. Underneath the shock of the truth of his words, she wondered just how much he had been able to see in her. She had never met a man who could sense so much about another person. She guessed his lonely life in the West had made him a deep thinker.

She was still contemplating later, during the celebration, when a commotion erupted to one side of the wedding celebration. The fiddle music stopped. Everyone turned to see. Elizabeth tried to get close enough to find out what was happening. Pushing her way through the crowd, she saw Jared raise his fist and punch a man in the face. He fell backwards. Another man ran for Jared, but Jeremiah grabbed him, pinning him to the ground. Jeremiah looked up, "Everything is under control. Looks like Jerry and Smith here just smuggled in a little whiskey. We'll take care of it." Jerry and Smith had been hired by Doc to carry supplies to the wagons from town and had been invited to stay for the wedding. Surely, they would be gone by morning.

Elizabeth shuddered, remembering the effects of liquor on another man long ago. She turned and ran as fast as her swollen body would let her. Elizabeth reached her wagon. She crawled under a worn quilt and finally allowed the sobs to escape her. A few minutes later she heard a voice.

"Elizabeth, honey, what's wrong?" It was Jessie.

"Nothing, guess that fight just scared me."

"Men always act ornery when they get too liquored up. That's why Jeremiah forbids it."

"I know. It just scares me. I remember. . . well I'm fine, really I am." Elizabeth could not bring herself to tell Jessie why the liquor scared her.

"Don't you want to come back to the dance? Music started again." Jessie asked.

"No, I'm tired. I guess I'll just go to sleep."

Jessie left, not prying any further into Elizabeth's despondency.

Elizabeth lay shivering for a long time before she could let sleep claim her exhausted mind and body.

# 7

## *Books*

"ELIZABETH, WHAT DO YOU plan to do when we get to Oklahoma Territory?" Jessie asked the next day as they gathered twigs on a hill outside of Russellville, Arkansas, for a fire.

"I just don't know, Jessie. I know I have to know soon. Jared told me in a couple of days we will reach Fort Smith. Then it'll just be waiting for the president to make up his mind about opening the lands." Elizabeth said.

"Well, I just wanted to tell you, you're more than welcome to stay with me and Amos, I'm sure he won't mind."

"I don't want to intrude, Jessie. I suppose I could get a job teaching or sewing."

"In your condition?" Jessie looked at her, eyes traveling to the part of her that expanded more every day.

"Well, the baby's got to come sometime. I'll just take her with me to school." Elizabeth had doubt in her voice.

"Yes, and what school board will stand for that?" Jessie chomped a new plug of tobacco. "You know most schools expect their teachers to be unmarried and a perfect example of purity. If you tell them you're unmarried, well, you have the baby, and if you tell them you're a widow. . ." Jessie shrugged and spat a stream of tobacco.

"I hear teachers are scarce out here. Hopefully they'll be glad to get me." Elizabeth turned on her heel and marched away, ending the conversation.

The conversation disturbed Elizabeth. She knew she was faced with a dilemma. She was sure her fellow travelers wondered why she had not married Sam. That would have been the easiest route. She just could not bring herself to marry someone for those reasons. Besides, her grief was too fresh, too painful for her to be joined to another. *What if Sam had found out the truth?*

When she walked into camp later that evening, she heard an excited buzz. "What's going on?" She asked Jessie as she approached their fire.

Jessie stood, wiping her hands on her worn calico apron, "I think it's time I lightened the load for the horses. Mayhap I should shed some of these books?"

Elizabeth was about to speak when Jared walked up. "Need a hand?"

"You can take this here trunk and leave it over there." Jessie pointed to the side of the road.

As he lifted the chest, grunting and groaning, Jared asked Jessie, "What do you have in this thing? Lead?"

"Books."

"Books?"

"I'm going to leave them. They were my late husband's. I kept them only because they reminded me of him. I think it's time to ease the load for these horses." Jessie said.

Jared opened a drawer. Elizabeth picked up a book.

"Lands, Jared, are you interested in them?" Jessie asked.

"I ain't never seen this many books in one place. They can't go to waste, they just can't." Jessie looked shocked.

"Well, you can put them in your own wagon! I'm done with the lot!"

Later that evening, Elizabeth walked past Jared's fire to see him staring at a book.

"What are you reading?" She asked, holding water buckets.

"Here, let me help you." He jumped up and grabbed the buckets. "You know you shouldn't be carrying this." He glanced at her round middle.

"I'm fine. What are you reading?"

"I don't rightly know."

"How can you not know what you're reading?" Elizabeth picked up the book. She tried to lean over, but could not because of her extra weight. He handed it to her.

"Plato's *Republic*, this is deep stuff, what are you reading philosophy for?"

"I wasn't."

"But you. . ."

"I can't read." Jared said.

"You can't?" Elizabeth looked surprised. "Then what are you doing with all these books?"

"I couldn't see good books without wanting them. We never had any book but the Bible at my house. And Ma never did take time to teach me how to read from it." Jared said.

"Well, I can teach you."

"You could?" Jared's eyes filled with hope.

"Of course I could. Let's start now. You have a slate? Of course not. Give me that stick. We'll scratch letters in the dirt." She lowered her swollen body down by the fire. Jared set the buckets down. Eagerly he watched as she scratched "ABC" into the dirt next to the fire.

"Where did you learn to read?" He asked.

"Mrs. Finch's School for Girls." Elizabeth smiled.

"Why the smile?"

"I hated that school! But I guess I learned some important things like reading. Walking down the stairs with a book on my head did not help me at all in the long run. Oh!"

"What's wrong?" He jumped.

"I'm fine. Just a rather hard kick."

"How long until that little one arrives?"

"Supposed to be born about May. I plan on being settled somewhere before then. Jared, what are you going to do if President Harrison decides not to open the land for settlement?"

"I refuse to think of that."

"Are you sure there will be enough land to go around? We keep passing more and more people bound for Oklahoma."

"If there's not enough, I will get mine through any way I can."

"What does that mean?"

"It means there are men sneaking into the territory and claiming it as theirs already. I can do the same."

"How do you know?" She asked.

"Heard."

"Heard what?"

"Just heard, that's all." Seeing she would get nowhere with that conversation, she shifted subjects.

"What are you going to do with your land when you get it? You don't seem the farmer type, you know with the barb wire fence and the red barn."

"Ranch."

"Ranch. Oh, that must be where your cute little cattle herd comes in." She moved her head towards the bovine community shaking their tails.

"Cute little cattle herd! Why those are prized beeves!" Jared's voice raised an octave. She had never seen him so excited.

"Sorry. I should've known that would bother you. You seem pretty attached to the animals."

"Attached!"

"Really, Jared. Hmm. Let's get back to the ABC's."

"Miss High and Mighty!"

"Well, I didn't ask for your majesty's opinion on my cattle!" Elizabeth could not believe him. He was truly offended by her comments. *I've never seen someone protective of a few livestock.*

"Do you want to continue with your reading lesson?" She asked.

"Not if you're going to lord it over me that you're better than me," he said.

"Really, Jared, I'm truly sorry about what I said about your cattle. Please calm down or I'm going to get mad." She put her hands on her hips and tapped her small foot.

Jared took a deep breath. The words began to tumble out of his mouth.

"I guess I did get a little touchy. But you can't understand. These 'cute little cows' have been like family to me. I had a huge herd up in Dakota Territory until last winter." He swallowed hard, Adam's apple bulging. She waited in silence.

"Blizzards came. You ain't never seen nothing like it. Snow blowing so hard you can't see your fist in front of your face. Railroads froze up. Couldn't get food into town. Me, well I holed up in my soddy. But the cattle, they had nowhere to go."

"You didn't have a barn?" Elizabeth asked in innocence.

"No barn big enough for 300 head."

"Oh." She nodded, encouraging him to go on.

He continued. "The blizzards started in October. By January all of my cattle were dead. Frozen. I managed to save ten head by cramming them into the stable with my horse. Those ten are what you see right over there."

"Oh, Jared, please forgive me. I realize more and more each day what a little life I led. I'm ashamed."

"Don't be. You didn't know." He studied his hands. The fire was nothing but coals.

"It must be late! I must get to bed."

"Yeah. You should get your rest." Jared stood up, holding out his hand. She took it. He walked her to her wagon, helping her in.

"Night, Elizabeth."

"Good night, Jared."

She curled up next to the flour sack, hugging her pillow, comforting herself with memories of his strong arm helping her into the wagon. *Oh Jared, the pain you've gone through. The loss you've had. If only I could take them all away.* For the first time since she had fled Virginia, she went to bed without frightening memories haunting her. Instead, she tried to pray for her friend. *God, where are you? Where were you when Jared's parents died? When his cattle froze? Where are you now? Can you hear me? Can you get Jared some land so he can be happy again?* The March winds blew. She huddled under her blankets, with nightmares of snow swirling around her.

# 8

# *Fort Smith*

THEY RODE INTO FORT Smith midmorning. Shocked at such a modern city rising up over the horizon, Elizabeth began to worry about her appearance. Maybe out in the hills it did not matter if one was covered in filth and pregnant, but here in society, it was a different matter. She hid under the canvas, eyes peeking out like a child in trouble. Jared rode behind her, on his horse, Emma driving his wagon. Every now and then she studied his face. She wished she could tell what he was thinking.

They pulled up in front of a store. Jeremiah jumped off his horse. "Ya'll stay here a spell. I'm going to go get us some food."

"He's buying for all of us?" Jessie asked Elizabeth.

"How would I know?" Elizabeth tried to brush the dirt off her dress. Jessie's gloved hands held tightly to the reins.

"Look at that hotel!" Elizabeth heard Emma's voice from Jared's wagon next to them. A huge brick building loomed in front of them, its sign in gold letters.

"What I wouldn't give for a long soak in a hot tub." Elizabeth said.

"Keep dreamin'" Jessie pulled a plug of tobacco out of her tin.

"Jessie, must you do that here?"

"What?"

"The tobacco."

"Girl, you worrying about what them folks out there think?" Jessie peered from under her broad brimmed straw hat.

"We already look bad enough, but a woman chewing. . ." Elizabeth said.

Just then Jeremiah appeared in the doorway of the store. His hands were empty.

"What is he doing?"

Jeremiah jumped on his horse, motioning for them to follow. At Jessie's "Giddup" the horses clop-clopped through the brick streets. They moved for a few blocks, Jeremiah hastening to a stop in front of the tallest, red brick, fanciest hotel on the block.

Jeremiah stopped his horse again, and disappeared behind the gilt-edged wooden doors. Elizabeth could hear the buzzing around her. They had been planning to purchase some food, and find a campsite outside of town. Instead they were stopped at a fancy hotel.

Finally, Jeremiah returned. He walked up to Jessie's wagon, motioning for Sam, Jared, George, and Doc to join him. "We're staying here."

"What? Now I know you's plum crazy!" Jessie roared. "Where we going to get the cash money for this?"

"We're guests. All expenses paid."

"Guests of whom? Queen Victoria?"

"Jessie, will you let the man talk?" Doc remarked, annoyed.

"I have an influential friend in this town. His name is Isaac Parker." Jeremiah put his thumbs in his belt loops and stepped back, his brown eyes dancing, as if waiting for his words to take effect.

The gasp was from Jared. Doc pounded Jeremiah on the back, exclaiming, "I knew it'd come in handy to know a fellow like you." The name made no impact on Elizabeth.

"Who is he?" she asked.

"Only the most famous judge the West has ever known." Jeremiah responded.

George piped in, "He's the cruelest, meanest man around."

"He ain't. That's just what you read in them Eastern papers." said Jeremiah.

"Then why is he called the 'Hanging Judge?'" George asked.

"Cause he does his job."

Jared said, "I don't want to be a guest of that man."

Jeremiah pointed west, down the hill. "Then you can go park your horse down there by the Arkansas River and roll your bedroll on the ground and freeze your tail off like we been doing for weeks. I aim to have some luxury." Jeremiah walked to his wagon, and began unloading his bags.

"Where are we going to put these wagons?" Jessie asked.

"Livery down the street." Jeremiah replied.

Elizabeth looked at Jared. He seemed truly disturbed. He must have a reason.

"Are you leaving, Jared?" asked Elizabeth as a bell boy took Jessie's trunk. Her eyes pled even if her words did not. *Please stay.*

Jared shrugged, dismounted, and walked his horse down the street. He had not answered, but she was in no mood to follow him. She gathered her scant belongings and rolled them in the worn quilt upon which she usually slept. She remembered the last time she had stayed in a hotel like this. She, Aunt Jane and Uncle Randall, once upon a time, had waltzed into the largest, most prestigious hotel in the nation's capital. Then she was adorned in pearls, a Parisian dress, and delicate white boots made in the softest kid leather. She was sure she had held a purple parasol in her gloved hands. Was that only a year ago? Surely, she had lived seven lifetimes since that day. As always, when she remembered the past, one face invaded her memory, making her heart jump, race, and her hackles raise as a cat scared of a dog. *William.*

Shaking her head, she shoved William's face into the farthest, darkest, shadowy part of her mind, and saw Jared walking back up the street. He must have been convinced that a hot bath and soft bed would feel good. As he neared the wagon, he offered his hand to help Elizabeth down. No one looked at Elizabeth's dress in admiration; in fact, a few peacock-like dames ruffled their feathers as she clopped past in her thick boots. She did not hold the glances against those women. She would have done the same last year. Head held high Elizabeth pretended she had the pride of a debutante about to descend her father's gilded, golden staircase. Instead of a parasol she held a reeking bedroll of unwashed clothing. Instead of a Parisian dress, she wore a calico rag that boasted three months of trail dust. Instead of her money-wielding relatives, she held the arm of a well-built cowboy; a cowboy that treated her better than her family ever had. And for that, she held her head high. Let the peacocks strut and the roosters crow. She had a friend, no, several friends, something that mattered more than money or fancy dresses.

Jared, Elizabeth, Jessie, Jeremiah, and Doc stood in front of the carved mahogany desk in the front of the hotel. Sam, Emma, and the two children stood back, as if in awe and afraid to approach the bench of the judge himself. George, Mildred, Becky and Jacob stood to one side. Rich, velvet carpet the color of a June rose covered the floor. Paintings in monstrous gold frames graced the beautifully papered walls. A mustached, short, round man handed them keys as soon as Jeremiah dropped the Isaac-Parker–magic–word.

Jessie and Elizabeth were to share a room. They trudged up the red velvety carpeted stairs, stopped in front of a door, and inserted a fancy key. The door opened, and Jessie entered, Elizabeth close behind. She looked around at the luxurious room. Yellow-flowered wallpaper covered the walls and thick gold carpeting swathed the floor. Elizabeth was sure all of the wood furnishings were the finest quality. She had never noticed the furniture at home, but she was sure it had been this nice. *There was nothing like being deprived to make one appreciate a little civilization.* She walked over to light a lamp. Just then a shriek from Jessie made her jump. She turned. Jessie had pulled back a beautiful yellow-gold curtain from the corner. Elizabeth rushed to touch the beautiful, long, luxurious bathtub.

"I'm going to go find out where we get water for this!" Jessie exclaimed. Elizabeth sat down on the bed and then jumped back up. She didn't want to make the bedspread as filthy as she was. She stood.

Jessie came back into the room, a young bellboy in tow. He had a bucket of hot water in his hand.

"I bring more." He left.

After several trips, the dirty little boy had filled the tub. Jessie looked at Elizabeth, "You can have your bath first. I'm going to look for Doc." She turned and left the room before Elizabeth could protest.

Elizabeth had just tugged her dress off when a knock sounded at the door.

"Yes?" she called as she tested the water of the gold-edged bathtub.

"Mrs. Duncan, it's Jeremiah."

"I'm sorry, could you come back later?"

"It's important."

"Give me a minute, then." She pulled her filthy dress back over her equally filthy curly, matted dark brown hair. She yanked open the door.

"Would you do the honor of allowing me to escort you to supper tonight?" He held his hat in his hands.

"What?" She wondered if she had heard him correctly.

"I'm asking you to accompany me to supper tonight."

She picked up her jaw off the floor. *Jeremiah? Asking me?* "Mr. Brown, I don't know." She hesitated. *What was his motive?* Suddenly, thinking of William, she was scared.

"Please. I'm having dinner with Judge Isaac Parker. I would like you to accompany me."

"Why?" she asked rudely.

"Why not?"

"I have nothing to wear. My clothes are in rags."

He pulled a roll of bills out of his back pocket. "Here, get you something nice."

"Mr. Brown—"

"I won't take no for an answer."

"Yes, you will." She slammed the door in his face.

"What's going on?" She heard Jessie's voice through the door.

"Mrs. Duncan is playing hard to get, I'm afraid."

"About what?"

"I asked her to supper."

Jessie noted the wad of cash in Jeremiah's hand. "Jeremiah Brown, you low down snake. You keep away from Elizabeth. She ain't one of them fancy ladies you can buy."

"I'm not trying to buy her! I just offered to buy her a dress to wear tonight."

"Jessie, tell him to leave!" Elizabeth yelled.

"Elizabeth, let me in!" Jessie eased herself through the cracked door.

"Now, will you tell me the meaning of this mess?" Jessie tossed her hat on the yellow bedspread and plopped herself down among the pillows. Elizabeth wished Jessie would have bathed and changed into fresh clothing first.

"He wants me to go to dinner with him and that Judge tonight."

"Why did you refuse the gentleman?"

"It's Jeremiah, Jessie. Why would he all of a sudden show me attention?"

"Well, even though he is old enough to be your pa, he ain't bad looking." Jessie winked.

"Jessie!"

"Just joshin' with you, Elizabeth. Wait, are you afraid?"

"Yes."

"This ain't William. Besides, you spend plenty of time with Jared. Maybe he'll wake up and smell the posies if he sees you with Jeremiah."

"Jessie, you are worse than a fourteen-year-old at her first dance!" Elizabeth stomped into the bathroom, and began pulling her dress over her head again. She eased her watermelon shaped body into the tub and jerked the curtain closed.

"What do you want me to tell Jeremiah?" Jessie called.

"Tell him *you'll* go with him!"

"No, I'm already going. Doc asked me. He's eating with the Judge tonight too."

"Why didn't you say so?" A splashing sound came from the direction of the tub. Elizabeth had dropped her soap.

"You didn't ask."

"I'll go if you go."

"You are impossible."

"You want I should tell Jeremiah?" Jessie asked.

"Yes! Now leave me in peace! It's been months since I had a bath! There must be layers of grime that will take hours to soak off." Elizabeth longed for a Jane Austen novel, but instead leaned back and shut her eyes.

"Jeremiah, you still out there?" Jessie yelled through the wooden door.

"Yeah."

"You crazy?" Jessie swung the door open.

"Naa, I'm just smoking a cigar waiting for one of you women to tell me what's going on." Jeremiah leaned back on the high heels of his boots, a thick brown cigar sending smoke in curls around his brown hair and his dirty unshaven face.

"She said she'd go."

"You ought to be a lawyer, Jessie. I'll tell Isaac you want a job."

"Oh, be gone with you, Jeremiah, but first give me that money." She shooed him with her hand.

"This ain't for you." But he handed it to her anyway.

"I know. But me and Elizabeth's going shopping."

Jeremiah handed over the bills. He rolled his eyes, flicking ashes on the carpet. He called over his shoulder as he loped down the hallway. "Tell her I'm picking her up at seven sharp."

"I will." Jessie returned to the room. She looked at the wad.

"Elizabeth, he must be sweet on you! He sure did you give you a wad of cash for just one dress!" she yelled across the room.

"Jessie, you can buy a new dress with it too. What he doesn't know won't hurt him."

"You're too generous. Hurry up in there. We need to get moving if we're going to be presentable for tonight."

"Oh pshaw!"

An hour later, Elizabeth and Jessie moved along the board-walk streets of Fort Smith. Elizabeth noted people of all walks of life sauntering along the streets. She even saw a few that she thought might be Indian, but one could not tell, they were dressed just like white people. She saw a few "painted ladies." Hearing the words "Riverfront Hotel" raised her curiosity.

"Jessie, have you heard about the Riverfront?"

"Yeah, just that Doc said to stay away from it. That made me curious as a cat in front of a mouse hole. It must be a bawdy house."

"Have you ever wanted to go in one of those just to see what it's like?"

"Nope."

As if hearing her words, a few "saloon girls" breezed past her. The smell of cheap perfume met Elizabeth's nose. The disdain she had been taught to hold for such women did not rise to her heart. Thinking of her past, she looked down at her belly and sighed. She suddenly felt intense pity for those women. Who knew the circumstances that had motivated them to seek such disdainful employment? Perhaps it had not been so different from her. . .

They had arrived at what looked like a dress shop. "Jessie, this looks a little expensive."

"We'll see."

They pushed the door open. The bell clanged. A grey-haired, mustached clerk looked up from a shiny countertop.

"May I help you?"

"We need dresses." Jessie blurted.

"Yes." His eyes darted to the part of Elizabeth's anatomy that bulged. The material was stretched to its limit. She pulled her worn coat around her tighter. It would not meet.

"Come this way." He directed them to a few racks of calico dresses.

"Don't you have anything nicer?"

"Yes." His "yes" said, *"I didn't think you could afford any better."*

"I am looking for something in red silk." Jessie said and then burst out laughing. Like they could afford silk. The man gave them a puzzling look.

"May I interest you in this red calico?" he asked. Jessie's eyes lit up.

"Where can I try this on?"

"In the back." Jessie disappeared through the rear door.

"Now, let's see what we have for you."

Elizabeth blushed. She wished she could just turn and run, but she must have a dress. She knew the one she was wearing wouldn't last much longer.

"I need black." She must keep up her facade as a widow.

"Black?"

"Yes, please."

He walked back to the calico rack. He pulled out a black calico with white sprigged flowers. "This is all I have."

She looked at it. It had no waist. It resembled, well. . . that tent that Sam and Emma set up for the children. But she looked at the rag she was wearing, a cast-off from Jessie. This would be better. *My aunt would die if she saw me in this. But then, she would die if she knew I was out shopping at this late date in my pregnancy.*

"I'll take it."

Jessie appeared. The dress fit her perfectly. She twirled, and then went back to change. The clerk wrapped their purchases securely in brown paper, tying them with white string.

\* \* \*

"Judge Parker, may I present Mrs. Duncan, Doctor Sims, and Mrs. Shows." Elizabeth had never heard so much pride in Jeremiah's voice. They all murmured polite greetings and were seated. Jeremiah gentlemanly seated Elizabeth in a high-backed chair. The hotel dining room was filled with a buzz of conversation. The smell of freshly cooked ham met Elizabeth's nostrils. She was starving.

Elizabeth's gaze took in Judge Parker. He must have been well over six feet tall, and over 200 pounds. His blue eyes pierced whatever he looked at, and his thick white hair and goatee gave him an intimidating presence. She would not want to cross this man. She wondered why Jared did not like him. Had Jared ever crossed him?

She was pulled back into the conversation.

"You ever hung an innocent man?" Doc asked the Judge. Elizabeth thought it rude of him.

"Never. It is my motto, 'No guilty man shall escape and no innocent man should be punished.'" Judge Parker looked at Elizabeth. She wondered if he saw her guilt.

"How are your wife and son?" asked Jeremiah.

"My son, Charles, is feeling poorly tonight, that is why my wife, Mary, could not join us."

"Oh, I hope he recovers soon," Jeremiah replied.

The waiter interrupted to take their orders. Elizabeth ordered a steak. She hesitated to be so extravagant, but she guessed if Jeremiah had invited, he would pay. Jessie had ordered a steak. It would taste so good after beans and cornbread of the past three months. She wondered what the Judge thought about dining with a pregnant lady.

"What do you suggest for a group going into Indian Territory?" Doc Sims asked as they received their food a few minutes later.

"Guns and ammunition." The Judge reached for the butter to spread on his roll.

"Because of the Indians?" Jessie asked.

"No, because of the outlaws. The territory is absolutely infested with them. The Indians won't bother you. They are civilized."

"Civilized? Indians?" Doc's thick eyebrows rose.

"Yes, the Five Civilized Tribes occupy most of the eastern half of the state. They have their own governments. I rarely have to settle anything between them. It's the white outlaws that occupy the territory that take all my time. There are 70,000 square miles out there that I take care of, and nary is a white man out there who has ever earned an honest buck."

"Sorry, Judge, but I ain't never heard of a civilized Indian," Doc said.

Jessie squirmed in discomfort. Elizabeth saw the corners of the Judge's mustache begin to pull toward the decorated ceiling. *Why he's almost handsome when he smiles.* "See that table over there." He moved his eye toward a well-dressed crowd two tables over. "Those are Indians. They are Cherokee, here in Fort Smith on business."

Elizabeth tried not to show her surprise. The training she had received at Mrs. Finch's came in handy every now and then. Out of the corner of her eye, she saw six men dressed in tailored suits. They were dark-skinned, but one of them had hair lighter than hers.

Judge Parker continued, "Easterners get the impression, via those dime paperback novels that the West is still full of painted chiefs on their palominos ready to scalp anything white that crosses their paths. That is not true. After being driven here over the Trail of Tears, many tribes set up their own form of government that frankly, I think works better than ours at times."

"But. . ." Doc stammered.

"But they don't look like Indians. Over the years many Indians have intermarried with white people. Many Indians have light skin, light hair, and even blue eyes, but they still claim full-fledged citizenship in their tribes." Judge Parker looked at Jeremiah, eyebrow slightly raised. Elizabeth took that to mean, *where in the world did you find this guy?*

Elizabeth crossed her knife and fork on the plate, a sign that the waiter could take it back to the kitchen. Jeremiah murmured, "Would you like dessert?"

"No, thank you," she whispered. He truly was playing the gentleman. She found herself wondering what his background was. So far, she had had no reason to be embarrassed over her pregnancy. The table hid her belly from the majority of the crowd. A feeling of gratitude to Jessie for convincing her to dine flowed through her veins, making her feel warm all over.

Over coffee, the conversation turned to the opening of the lands, as it always did. Elizabeth tried not to fidget. She was so uncomfortable and kept thinking of the soft bed upstairs. She wanted to ask how far they must travel into Indian Territory to arrive at the edge of the unclaimed lands. Should she? *Go for it*, her mind told her.

"Judge Parker, how far is it to the place where the lands are not claimed?" Her voice shook just a little.

His blue eyes grabbed hers. A twinkle shone. "About 190 miles."

"That far?" she asked, "And here I thought we had arrived at the edge of Indian Territory."

"You have. But the lands on this side are still Indian lands."

Jeremiah patted her hand, "Don't worry, Mrs. Duncan, we'll get you safely through." She heard confidence in his voice, but it did not help matters. She had spent all this time being afraid of the Indians, only to find it was not necessary to be afraid of them. But she had to be afraid of the outlaws, white men, hiding from the law across the Arkansas River. She longed for safety. Would she ever have someone again tell her she was safe, as her Papa had done so long ago? She wanted to discuss everything with Jared. Somehow, he made her feel better.

"I highly advise you do not attempt to cross Indian Territory." Judge Parker said.

"Now, Judge," Jessie exonerated, "we got plenty of guns and we all can shoot. We took care of some no-accounts a few weeks ago and we'll do the same again."

Doc, for once, nodded in agreement at Jessie's remarks. Jeremiah offered, "I hear the president could sign the bill at any moment. We simply do not have time to go around Indian Territory."

"What do you mean go around it?" asked Elizabeth. "Where would that path lead us?"

Judge Parker leaned back in his chair. "I recommend you travel north through Arkansas to Kansas, go West, and then enter Oklahoma Territory from the north.

"But we will lose three or four days travel that way, Judge!" exclaimed Doc.

"What you will gain is the protection of civilized country. You do not understand how dangerous Indian Territory is to the traveler."

Doc, Jeremiah, and Jessie continued to argue with the Judge until Elizabeth was shocked at their sharp words. Finally, they agreed to discuss it in the morning since the clock was striking ten. The Judge excused himself, bowing politely to the women, and walked out of the dining room, head high, shoulders back, as if he owned the world.

Jeremiah escorted Elizabeth to her room, and then left for his quarters. Doc and Jessie had begged their leave. Elizabeth was sure now that Jessie and Doc were romantically intertwined. Well, that was Jessie's business.

Weariness settled deep into her bones. Did she want another bath? No. She was restless despite her exhaustion. Here in the dark room, thoughts of another outlaw raid made her bite her nails. Maybe she would go downstairs and find a magazine to read.

Coming down the intricately carved staircase she had just ascended, she saw several more Indians. They, too, were dressed well. Sounds of saloon music floated through the thick brick walls. Obviously, most people in this town felt ten o'clock too early to retire. She walked over to the desk to ask about a magazine. *Maybe they have Godey Lady's Book,* thought Elizabeth. How long had it been since she had seen one of those? Not as long as it felt like.

They did have one. She grabbed it and turned to go up the stairs. She took one step at a time, slowly adjusting her weight. Arriving at her room, she settled herself on the bed. Turning on the ornate lamp, she opened the pages. This very copy she had in her room in Virginia. She had spent hours going over the fashions and reading the stories. Now the same stories bored her. The writers had no idea of life outside their safe, Eastern homes. Closing her eyes, she remembered her new spring suit, a white organdy, with flowing lace, and just the right sized bustle. She had a parasol to match it. She had seen one just like it in this book, and her aunt's seamstress had sewn it for her, and she had worn it to Washington City. Once she had been fashionable. She laughed and tossed the magazine on the floor, bored. *I need some sleep.*

She rolled over, still fully clothed, and the yellow room soon faded into the background. Her eyelids closed.

# 9

## *Illness*

ELIZABETH WOKE TO FIND Jessie sleeping next to her. She had a bandage around her head. *How did I sleep through her coming in?* She tried to get out of the bed without waking her, but Jessie stirred, moaning.

"Ooh, my head feels like a train hit it."

"What happened to you last night?"

"You probably don't want to know, Lizzie." Elizabeth put her hands on her hips.

"Just a little scratch." Jessie tried to get to her feet and stumbled.

"D—did you drink some whisky?" Now Jessie had gone too far.

"Na, nothing like that, girl, Doc and me, well, we. . ."

Elizabeth, hands on her hips, tapped her foot, "And. . .?"

"We were trying to paint the canvas on the wagon to say, 'Oklahoma or Bust,' and I fell off the side and hit my head. Ooh." She put her hand to the bandage on her head and moaned again.

"Well, I certainly hope Doc did something about it since it was his fault!"

"It wasn't his fault. It was all my idea. He wrapped it up and gave me some powders he had in his bag." Jessie had managed to stand and tried to walk to the washbasin. She gazed at herself in the mirror and noted a purple eye and a bulging lump under the bandage.

"Girl, looks like I got into a scrape. I'll tell the others I fought off some outlaws."

"Really, Jessie, you and your hair-brained ideas! Whatever possessed you to paint the wagon canvas?"

"Saw some other folks coming through town with theirs painted. Didn't want us to feel left out."

Someone knocked on the door. Jeremiah's voice called through the wooden barrier. "Hey, you womenfolk awake yet? Rooster done crowed an hour ago!"

Since she was already dressed, Elizabeth yanked open the door. "Mr. Brown, Jessie's been hurt."

"Whatever happened?"

"I'll let Doc tell you, but she is not in any condition to travel!"

"Jessie's got a constitution of steel. She'll be fine." Then he saw Jessie's bruised face. "Lands, Jess, what did you do? Fight off a bear?"

"I ain't telling you nothing! Lizzie, get him outta here."

"No need, I'm leaving." He left. Elizabeth shut the door.

"Jessie, didn't you hear Judge Parker say last night that President Harrison was going to sign the bill sooner than we thought? We gotta get moving! You knew that! Why did you take such a risk?"

"Girl, go get Doc, I'm sick." Then she lost her supper all over the washbasin, carpet, and Elizabeth's shoes.

Elizabeth helped Jessie back to the bed, took off her soiled shoes, and ran, or rather, waddled, down the hall to Doc's room. She banged on the door.

"I'm comin'! Hold your horses!"

"Doc, it's Jessie, she's vomiting."

"I'm coming."

He grabbed his black bag and followed Elizabeth down the hall. Elizabeth could hear Jessie vomiting again as they came to the doorway of their room.

"Now, now, then, Jessie." Doc was surprisingly tender.

Elizabeth took a towel and tried to mop the mess. It was difficult to get to her knees, but she had to. As soon as she got to her knees, she lost her own supper. Doc dropped a few expletives and jumped back, but vomit covered *his* shoes now.

"Elizabeth?" He asked.

"I'm fine. It's just my. . . condition." Elizabeth sat back on her heels and wiped her face. Doc walked to the door and yelled, "Hey, some help in here, please!"

In a few seconds, a servant boy came running. Doc barked some orders and the boy started cleaning the vomit. Doc helped Elizabeth to her feet and then helped her lie down next to Jessie on the bed. Jessie only moaned.

"Do you feel dizzy, Jess?" asked Doc.

"The room is spinning if that's what you mean." Jessie had no color in her face save the bruised eye.

"Now, Jessie, you got a concussion. You are going to have to stay still at least a day."

"A day? We got to get moving, Doc!"

"Nope. You stay put!" He reached for the glass on the nightstand, filled it with water from the pitcher near the washbasin and mixed a powder into it.

"Here, this'll help with the pain." He held Jessie's head while she sipped the mixture.

Elizabeth had never felt so weak in her entire pregnancy. Perhaps she had allowed everything to catch up now that they were in a comfortable and safe place, perhaps she had let herself feel the misery at last. She closed her eyes.

Doc said, "For Pete's sake, girls, you done a doozy. We are going to have to stay put. I'm going to go find Jeremiah and get him to work some magic with Judge Parker for us to stay another night. Then I'm going to get Emma to come tend to you."

"But she's got her young'uns. . ." protested Jessie.

"We're fine," said Elizabeth.

"For once, you, Jessie, are going to do what I say. And as for you, Elizabeth, you should never have started this journey in the first place!" He marched across the wood floor, heels pounding, and then he closed the door firmly. Elizabeth, angry at what the Doc at said, moaned, but held an inner resolve to be better in a day.

"I do believe he meant what he said." Jessie tried to chuckle but ended up moaning.

Elizabeth rolled over to her left side and cried softly to herself. Then she slept.

* * *

A cool rag on her head brought Elizabeth back to reality. Emma's soft blue eyes peered at her.

"Haven't we been here before?" Elizabeth cracked a tiny grin.

"We do seem to play this role over and over." Emma's soft laugh comforted Elizabeth once more.

"Where's Jessie?" asked Elizabeth, referring to the empty side of the bed.

"She woke up feeling a little better and I sent her down to the dining room to get a bit of soup."

"She was walking?"

"Yes. Seemed fine."

"Ooh." Elizabeth clutched her belly as a strong cramp hit her.

"Now, Lizzie, do you have any idea when that baby of yours is supposed to be born?"

The room spun, and Elizabeth turned her head and vomited again. "Sometime at the beginning of May's best I can guess." She said as soon as she could speak again.

Emma rang the bell cord near the door to call a maid to clean. "Isn't that something? I never had anyone to clean up after me," laughed Emma.

"Well, darlin' it could be your time. It's March and babies come early."

"Oh, Emma, I'm so not prepared for this, but at least we are not in the wagon."

"Nothing to do but wait, child. If it's your time, nothing we can do about it, nor stop it."

Amazingly, Elizabeth woke a few hours later having had no more contractions. She was relieved. It was too early for a healthy baby, and she was not ready. The baby kicked as if in response to her thoughts. "You just stay put, baby." She shoved all the worried thoughts about having the baby on the trail to the back of her mind. Looking to the window, she saw it getting dark outside. Had she slept all day? She looked around the room and saw no one. Sitting, she wiped her face with her sleeve and tried to get to her feet. As she did, the door opened. Jessie and Emma entered.

"Girl, get your head back on that pillow!" Jessie gently pushed her back.

"But, Jessie, you're the one that was injured and sick."

"I'm fine now. Doc says I just need to take it easy."

"You should be in this bed too."

"Where I'm headed. Emma, you go tend to your young'uns, I got Lizzie."

Emma turned without a word and headed out the door. Jessie rang the bell. When the boy appeared, she told him to get Elizabeth some soup. He acted like he did not understand so she pantomimed until he nodded. She helped Elizabeth to her feet and took her to the washroom across the hall. When they returned, Elizabeth swallowed a few bites of soup, took a sip of water and fell back on the bed. Jessie looked in the mirror, swore under her breath at her face, and then took off her shoes and dress and collapsed into bed.

# Part Three

# *Indian Territory*

March 1889

# 10

# *Aenohe*

ELIZABETH LOOKED AROUND FOR snakes before settling down to
build a fire. Even though Jared had said it was still too cold for
snakes, one could never be too careful. Over the past week, Jessie
had recovered well. One could barely see the bruises anymore.

Their group had dwindled as Mildred and her family and the
others had decided passing through Indian Territory too dangerous. They had gone directly north, remaining in Arkansas, and said
they would head west once they arrived safely in Kansas. They had
only five wagons now: Jeremiah's, Doc's, Jared's, Sam's, and Jessie's.

They passed a few towns, populated almost entirely of Indians. These Indians did not meet the stereotype of any Indians
in books or stories she had read. Jared had stayed away from the
towns; this reminded Elizabeth about his hatred of Indians. At
least he wasn't causing trouble. She found the Indians quite pleasant, and most were dressed much nicer than any of the travelers.
She often wondered what they thought of all these whites traveling
through their land. So far no one had challenged them, although
Elizabeth wondered if what they were doing was legal. She guessed
that Judge Parker would have told them if it were not.

As she heated the coffee to go with their cold corn muffin breakfast, she saw Jared riding off in the distance. They were

camped next to the Canadian River, as they did most nights. They were following the river west. Jared crossed the river, his horse splashing through the shallow ford. The sun caught some of the water sprays, causing Elizabeth to think it the most beautiful site she had ever seen. Sometime yesterday she had realized the landscape had changed. Flat prairie spread out in every direction. Jessie complained about the barrenness of the land, but Elizabeth loved it. She felt freer than she had in her entire life. She watched Jared closely, although they had little time to talk. Jared was in his element. He smiled more; he laughed. He tossed his head back so far to chuckle sometimes that his hat fell off his head. Jessie and Doc's bantering kept Jared in stitches. Elizabeth often didn't think it funny, but she laughed when Jared did. His laugh was contagious.

So far, they had seen no bands of outlaws as Elizabeth had dreaded. Besides some farmhouses that were few and far between, they had seen nothing but the three Indian towns. Elizabeth was surprised they had not seen more people journeying towards Purcell, where most would wait for the opening of the lands. She guessed most took trains or went around Indian Territory.

Jared, she knew, rode with his ever-ready gun in his holster, as he "scouted" the for the next day's trek. This dry, open, and empty land made the Arkansas landscape look heavily populated. She prayed that Jared would come back to them safely.

As she prayed, she realized that she had been praying much more lately. Maybe it was the land? She felt close to the Creator out here in the midst of such beauty.

Emma called her good mornings from the midst of chasing Johnny away from the river. He loved to stamp his feet in the shallow pools at the edge of the riverbank. Emma had threatened to tie him to a picket line. His shoes took days to dry. Since they were his only pair, he must wear them wet. Emma constantly worried that Johnny would catch a cold, but the little tyke seemed to be full of health.

"Good Morning, Mrs. Duncan," Jenny called from in front of the LeBeau wagon. She stirred something in a bowl. Elizabeth knew it was corn muffins. They were so sick of the same fare day after day.

"Good morning, Jenny." She called cheerfully.

After doing the dishes and reloading the wagons, as they loaded the wagons to begin the day's journey, Elizabeth overhead Doc tell Jeremiah, "We've got to move on without him."

She knew they spoke of Jared. Usually, he returned from his wanderings before they left for the day. Bringing a finger to her mouth, she chewed. A nail. A nail had grown over the past week! She must be enjoying herself, but now she worried for Jared.

"Move out!" Jeremiah's voice boomed through the morning stillness. A fresh breeze blew in Elizabeth's face as she sat in her driver's position. Jessie crawled up to sit beside her. The March sky held fluffy white clouds that chased each other through the blue vastness. The wagon rolled and bumped beneath them.

At noon, they had not run into Jared. Jeremiah mentioned that he had seen tracks along the river, so they were following Jared's trail. Sam volunteered to ride ahead and search, but Jeremiah wouldn't hear of it. "Jared knows this land. He'll be fine."

*Jared knew this land? I thought he was from Kansas and Dakota Territory of late. I must ask Jeremiah about this.*

After their noon meal, Elizabeth trudged through the red sludge of the riverside to Jeremiah's wagon. He lay stretched out; his head propped against the wooden spokes of a rear wheel. His hat was over his face; his chest rose and fell evenly. Elizabeth hated to wake him but did anyway.

"Mr. Brown," She said.

"Whaa, oh. . ." he sat up, catching his hat in his left hand.

"Yes, Mrs. Duncan."

"I'm concerned about Mr. Davidson."

"Like I said he knows this country."

"He could know it while running into a bunch of ruffians."

"What do you want me to do?" Jeremiah pulled himself to his feet, his pointed toe boots leaving heavy marks on the soft ground.

"Find him."

"Mrs. Duncan, Jared has driven cattle through this territory up the Chisholm Trail and the Santa Fe Trail since he was fourteen years old. He knows every hideout, every nook and cranny, every cave in the bank of this river. I couldn't find him if I tried."

She hadn't known that. "What is he doing?"

"He's looking for a safe trail for us."

"Safe? Humph." She turned to walk away. She knew she had been rude but was sick of playing the nice polite lady when it came to getting information. She probably should have turned on the charm with Jeremiah. But she was afraid of encouraging him after he had taken her to dinner.

She chewed a nail as she watched Jenny chase Johnny away from the river. Sam paced in front of his wagon. They heard hoofbeats.

One horse.

Jared.

Elizabeth let out a sigh. She wanted to scream at him, to pound his chest with her fists for making her worry so. Why did she care what happened to him? She once again climbed over the wheel of her wagon. Jessie lay sleeping under the canvas. She noted Jared talking to Jeremiah. She waited for Jeremiah's voice to yell for them to move out.

Instead, Jared rode towards her. As he got closer, she saw a body lying in front of him across the horn of his saddle. A child's body.

"Jared! Who is that?" He pulled up next to her wagon.

"A hurt Indian boy. I need to put him in your wagon. It's the only one with room."

"Jessie's under the wagon, let's ask her."

Jessie popped her head up. "I'm getting up. Jared, bring him back to this pallet here." Elizabeth could feel the motherly vibes flowing from Jessie. *Another orphan to take in. Like me.*

"Doc!" Jessie belted out. "Get over here and check out this boy!"

Doc sauntered over and stuck his head in the back of their wagon. A boy of about twelve years, clad in filthy buckskin with long black hair that had once been shiny lay on the faded patch-work. He looked—dead.

"Is he alive?" asked Elizabeth.

"Yeah." Doc leaned over him, prying the boy's eyes open. The LeBeau children had gathered around the quilt. Emma, Sam, and Jeremiah had joined them also. "Get back." Doc barked as usual. They all took a halfhearted step back.

"He's fine. Just starving." Doc pronounced as he straightened his back. "Get me some water, and you, Jessie, see if there's any dried beef left you can boil for some broth."

"I've got some here." Jared pulled a stick from the pocket of his rough leather jacket. Jessie, her worn gray skirts swaying, ran to bank the fire and put some water on to boil.

Elizabeth felt tiny fingers in her hand. Jenny looked up; her big brown eyes full of fear. "Is he going to scalp us?"

"No, Jenny, he's a nice boy. You'll see." Elizabeth wondered what a young boy was doing all alone in the middle of the prairie. *Where was his family? Where were those nicely dressed Indians?*

Jessie had some broth ready faster than Elizabeth believed possible. Doc had wandered back to his own wagon. Jared took the boy in his arms as gently as a mother would a newborn babe. He tilted the boy's head back and dropped some broth into the boy's mouth. It dribbled out. Jared tried again. This time Elizabeth saw the child swallow. A cheer rose up from everyone. Jared continued until the broth was gone.

Jeremiah said, "All right, folks, let's get moving before dark comes."

They all moved to their posts. Elizabeth heard Doc arguing with Jessie. "You can't keep an Injun boy in your wagon! What if his family comes looking for him? They'll think you kidnapped him!"

Jessie climbed onto the wagon seat. "Doc, you get over there to drive Jared's wagon and get your nose out of my business!"

"I can't believe Jeremiah let an Indian into this group!"

"He's a harmless, sick child!" Jessie yelled.

"He's a thieving, stinking, murdering polecat of an Injun! Let him die!"

"Doc Sims! You, a doctor! I thought you took an oath to care of folks, not to want them dead!" Jessie was livid. Elizabeth clicked her tongue to the horse she was driving. Doc was left standing by himself. Then he ran to jump on his own wagon seat and pulled his horses next to Jessie and Elizabeth's wagon. Jared pulled his horse up.

"Doc, get to your place behind them!"

"Shut up, Jared!"

"Doc, get back in your own spot. The boy stays! Now get behind them!" Jessie screamed. Elizabeth could hear Jared's cows bellowing.

"Doc!" Jared moved to take care of his cattle. His soothing voice brought goosebumps to Elizabeth's neck. He started singing a song to quiet them. Doc moved the wagon to its proper position. When things returned to the routine of the bumping, moving wagon, Elizabeth's thoughts wandered. She remembered Jared's hatred of Indians. *Why had he saved an Indian child?*

As the sun made its bed on the flat Western horizon, Elizabeth asked Jessie to watch the fire and walked over to Jared's wagon. While their meager meal of beans warmed over the coals, she would talk to Jared about the Indian boy who had just awakened. Jessie hovered over him. He was still too weak to say much or cause any trouble.

Jared sat mending a harness. She watched him as he bent over the leather straps. His hat covered his face. But she could see in her mind's eyes the concentration etched across his brow. The sweat dripped off his forehead in spite of the cool weather.

"Jared. May I sit down?"

"Yeah." He didn't look up. She lowered herself down next to him. He would have to help her up later. It was getting harder and harder to get around with her child getting heavier. A strong kick reminded her the time moved closer to that coming day.

"What happened out there? Where did you find the boy?" He finally finished his task, put the harness down, and gave her his full attention. The dusk provided just enough light for her to see the green flecks of his liquid eyes as he adjusted his hat.

"I found him next to the river in a hollowed part of a bank, face down in the mud. I thought he was dead." Concern filled his eyes like a father speaking of his own sick child.

"But—Jared, excuse me for asking—but did you realize he was Indian?"

"Yeah, that's why I had my gun drawn."

"And you helped him anyway?" she asked.

"When I felt his heart still beating, man, I thought, this is just a boy, I can't leave him out for the vultures."

"But you said you hated. . ."

He interrupted, "I told you I hated Indians. Yeah, I know. Somehow that hate didn't figure in the picture for a young'un."

Elizabeth saw Emma at the next wagon. She stirred her evening meal in its iron pot. Elizabeth knew Emma could not have helped but overheard their conversation, but Emma's grayish blonde head didn't once give away that fact. Suddenly Elizabeth wanted Emma to be a part of this conversation. She had spoken of God, of faith—the only one in the group who seemed to mention the subjects. What would Emma have to say to Jared about his hatred?

"Good evening, Emma," Elizabeth called.

"Nice night, isn't it?" Emma turned her head. The soiled apron covering her red calico blew in the wind.

"Why don't you take a break and sit down for a minute?"

Perhaps Emma heard the pleading in Elizabeth's voice. She came. She sat. And Emma never did that while preparing supper. Jared didn't seem to mind. *How do I do this?* Elizabeth wondered.

It didn't matter, for at that moment, Jessie's voice called across the camp. "Jared!" Excitement filled her voice.

Jared leaped to his feet, flying to answer Jessie's request. Emma stopped to pull Elizabeth to her feet, and they followed him. Emma called over her shoulder to Sam to watch the children.

The boy, obviously feeling better, had climbed over the wagon box, and had fallen in a heap behind it. Jessie, beside herself, sought to revive him. *Where was the Doc?* Once again, Elizabeth noted how Jared tenderly cared for the child. Dark, fear-filled eyes opened. The child tried to bolt again. Jared's arms held steady.

"Don't worry. We're friends." Jessie promised.

"What's your name?" Jared asked.

"Aenohe." It sounded like "Ah–no," but Elizabeth later learned the true spelling and that it meant "hawk."

"Well, Aenohe, I'm Jared, this is Jessie, Emma, and Elizabeth." The scared-rabbit-look in Aenohe's eyes told Elizabeth fear still gripped the child. "We're not going to hurt you." Jared continued.

"Why were you all alone out there?" asked Elizabeth.

"Where's my grandmother?" The child spoke perfect English.

"I'm sorry, Aenohe, but she's dead." Jared smoothed the hair off Aenohe's forehead.

"But. . .." His eyes closed again.

They tiptoed away to whisper. Emma said, "Jared, what could have happened?"

"I saw tracks around him when I picked him up. Someone shot his grandmother, and must have thought the boy was already dead."

"Why would someone shoot an old woman?" Jessie asked.

Jared shrugged and turned to go. Elizabeth read the pain on his face, but did not know what to say to him.

The next morning, they loaded the boy back into Jessie's wagon and moved along. Jessie drove. Elizabeth decided to ride in the back with the boy. He did not open his eyes much. She kept dripping broth into his mouth, and he would swallow, drip by drip. His poor stomach could not take much at a time. She could see the outline of his skull clearly. This boy had been without food for way too long.

At their noon stop, Jared rode over to check on Acnohe. He poked his head inside the back flap of the wagon and asked how Aenohe was doing. Elizabeth's look told him nothing had changed.

Two days passed in much the same manner. Elizabeth and Jessie took turns driving and riding with Aenohe. Emma sat with him when they stopped if Sam could mind the children. Jeremiah and Doc kept their distance, as if they were afraid of catching some mysterious disease from the boy. Jared showed so much concern and compassion Elizabeth had to chase him away.

On the third day after they found him, Aenohe could finally sit up without fainting. He seemed ready to talk, so Jared began some gentle probing. "Do you remember what happened before I found you?"

"No."

"Your grandmother was with you?"

"Yes."

"Why were you and your grandmother out here by yourselves?"

"Just were."

"Now look, Aenohe, we can't help you if you don't tell us the truth."

Aenohe's eyes looked defiant, but he relaxed and began his story. "We were running away."

"From what?"

He looked at Jared. "Government officials. My grandma and me, we didn't bother anyone. We lived away from farms and towns just like our Cheyenne ancestors lived. She is a medicine woman. I hunted jackrabbits, and we made it." He paused, taking a deep breath. "But then one day these officials came and told us I had to go to their school. I said I already knew English, why did I have to go to school? But they said I had to learn more. Grandma said they wanted to make me white, even though it was an Indian school. So we ran away."

"And that's the last thing you remember?" Jared asked softly. Elizabeth sat in the background, the only observer to the conversation.

"Yes." The boy closed his eyes again. They decided to leave him alone. Elizabeth saw Jared lean back on his heels and close his eyes tightly. He grimaced, then got to his feet and walked away. He kept walking until he came to the river, about ten feet from their camp. He sat. Every now and then he would toss a stone into the river.

No one bothered him. As Elizabeth got up to finish her chores, she noticed his shoulders shaking. *Was he crying? Should I go to him?* She remembered the time Jared had held her as she cried. She remembered his looks of compassion and friendship thrown across camp to her eyes. She knew that somehow, he had shared with her of his life, deep from his heart. She must go to him. *Wait, he was walking away!* Elizabeth watched his strong shoulders still shuddering. She knew he was trying to get away before anyone noticed his sobs. Throwing down her dishtowel, she went after him.

In her advanced stage of pregnancy, Elizabeth could not catch him. Finally, he sat down on a large rock on a bank high above the river. The red mud covered his boots *and my shoes,* she noted, as she silently crept up to him. She placed her hand on his wide shoulder. He did not look up, but placed his hand over hers.

Elizabeth found a rock next to his and sat down. The brisk March wind whistled through the few cottonwoods around them. The muddy red water churned in its springtime state. Elizabeth shivered and wondered how Jared did not shiver as well in his thin leather coat.

"Jared. . ." *What should I say?*

Finally, his hazel eyes found hers. The deep pools of green spilled over, like a high tide creeping up a beach, and wetting his weeks' growth of beard. She had never seen a man cry. Never. It frightened her.

"What's wrong?" she ventured. "Is it the boy?"

He doubled over. Sobs so loud filled the air and covered the sound of the river rushing. Pain, deep pain poured from the chasms of his soul where he had buried it long ago.

Reacting on instinct, Elizabeth did what she would have done if little Johnny had been crying. She leaned over, and wrapped her arms around him. Without saying anything, she held him as she felt his body shudder.

Finally, whispers met her ears through the roar of the river. He sat up.

"That boy, that boy. He's me."

Then she remembered him telling her of his parents killed by Indians in Kansas so long ago. He had been about the age of Aenohe, she recalled.

"Elizabeth, it was soldiers that killed his grandmother."

"How do you know?"

"The tracks. Those horses were shod by army blacksmiths. I also found this." He handed her a hat; the dark blue and black colors of a U.S. Army officer.

"But why would the army do that?"

"It's the law those Indians have to go to school to learn to fit in."

"Why didn't you tell us sooner?"

"I didn't want to bring it up. Elizabeth, that boy is a member of the Cheyenne tribe. This land we're sitting on is either Creek or Choctaw. Do you realize how far away he is from his own land? They must have run for a long time."

They sat in silence for what seemed like ages. She did not know what to say. She waited for him to continue. The questions raced through her mind like a stampede of cattle.

Finally, he spoke. She met his green eyes and looked deeply into them. She felt as if he had opened his soul to her. "I said I'm that boy because—of my parents. I told you about them. They were killed by Indians. I was that age. That same scared look haunted my eyes for years. The fear turned to hate, hate to bitterness. But I think maybe I've realized that—Indians hurt too and it's not always about being white or Indian. Hatred kills people."

"Oh Jared, I'm so sorry." She still had her arms wrapped around him. She heard a hawk call out overhead. The sky began to darken with the promise of a storm.

He stood and pulled her to her feet. He had revealed so much of himself to her. *Why? Why does he trust me? Do I trust him?* Oh, how she wanted to trust. But the pain of her past chained her heart.

Time stood still. He pulled her close, as close as her belly would let him. The baby kicked. In her ear, his husky voice whispered, "Thank you." Then he released her. He stared into her eyes and then his lips barely touched hers. They started back to camp, trudging through the red mud, skirting around the huge rocks deposited by the rushing waters. The smell of the dying fire reached her nostrils; a comforting odor, almost like a welcome home. Home? Was this new and wild land becoming home?

# 11

# *Wondering*

AENOHE GRADUALLY BEGAN TO gain weight and become more aware of his surroundings. Jared, Jessie, and Elizabeth talked about what to do about him. They had decided to let him stay with them for the time being. Aenohe attached himself to Jared, following him around like a faithful puppy. Jared didn't seem to mind. Jeremiah and Doc still skirted the issue and the boy. Elizabeth could feel tension in the air whenever one of them was around. She waited for the explosion over the matter that was bound to take place.

That morning, they came upon a wagon half-buried next to the river. Jeremiah called out a halt. They made camp a little early for the noon meal, but they didn't question, glad for the rest. Elizabeth saw Jared riding out ahead. If she wasn't so curious, she would have just eaten, as Aenohe and Jessie were doing. But she had to poke her nose into the matter. She just had to.

Pulling a shawl around her huge belly, she nonchalantly moved towards Jeremiah and Jared. When Jared looked up from the wagon, he hollered, "Back up, Elizabeth! This here's quicksand!" She jumped back, as much as a pregnant woman could jump.

"Just stay there, Elizabeth!" Jeremiah yelled.

"Alright, I'm staying! What are you looking at?" She bit at the nail on her left thumb.

"Never mind." Jeremiah flicked his fingers at her. That made her mad. Oh, how it made her mad!

She waited, pacing back and forth in front of them. Finally, Jeremiah walked over to where she paced. Jared still poked among the remains of the wagon.

"Found some dead folks."

"D-dead people?"

"Yeah, looks like they got stuck in the quicksand."

"This sounds like a dime novel, Jeremiah."

"Quicksand is real. Very real."

Emma walked up. "Dead?" she asked.

"Yep."

She walked away. The sound of children's laughter floated to Elizabeth's ears. *Laughter? With all this death around, how can they laugh? Death, death, death, I can't stand another death!* She turned from the horror of the scene, wanting to run. But there was nowhere to hide on the plains.

She caught up to Emma who turned toward her and said, "Sad, ain't it? They were probably on their way to get land like we are."

"Yes, it's sad." Suddenly, Elizabeth blurted, "Emma, how can God let this happen? How can he let so many innocent people suffer and die? And–and–How could he let William do this to me?"

Looking at Emma, Elizabeth remembered meeting the kind woman for the first time.

* * *

They arrived at 1:00 in the morning. Jessie pounded on the door of Emma's Nashville home, swearing that her sister would welcome them. Upon opening it, Emma found Jessie and Elizabeth outside, shivering in the cold. Jessie pushed Elizabeth forward into the house.

"This is Elizabeth Lee."

"How do you do?" Elizabeth's teeth chattered, hitting together like a hen clucking at her chicks. "Lands, child, come in and get warm." Emma pulled them both in. "What are you doing in Nashville, Sister, and at this time of night?"

"Our train arrived in Nashville an hour ago. We didn't have anywhere else to go."

"So you walked here? Why didn't you get a ride here?"

"We are fresh out of cash."

"You could have frozen to death!" Emma scolded. Jessie had always been the impulsive and emotional one in the family; Emma the strong and practical one. When Jessie had wired that they were on their way to Oklahoma Territory, Emma had asked that they stop and see her. The "they" being Jessie and a vagrant child she had written about.

Emma inspected Elizabeth closely. She was in the family way all right. She guessed about five months along. Remembering the difficulty of her own pregnancies, she wondered how Elizabeth had endured sitting in a slow-moving train for so long.

She wrapped a blue granny-square afghan around Elizabeth's shivering shoulders. Elizabeth could hear Emma's speak under her breath. But most of all she smelled food. She was starving.

"Poor, poor dear." Jessie had wired only a bare minimum of details concerning Elizabeth. Elizabeth knew that Emma knew that Jessie had been a cook in Elizabeth's family's home in Alexandria, Virginia, and that Jessie and Elizabeth had fled in a hurry. She could tell that Emma's curiosity was rising like a child peeping into a candy shop window, but gratefully Emma held her tongue. They would tell her their stories in time. Right now they all needed sleep.

"Thank you," Elizabeth said when Emma handed her a china cup of tea.

"So, you are on your way to an adventure?" Emma asked.

Jessie piped in, "You might call it that." She chuckled.

"Jessie, now where exactly did you get this hair-brained idea?" Emma asked.

"Could we maybe eat before I tell you? We are famished."

"Of course, forgive me." Emma moved to the stove, removed a pan, and dipped what looked like chicken soup into some bowls.

She handed Elizabeth and Jessie the bowls and put on a kettle for tea. After Jessie had inhaled the satisfying nourishment, she continued her explanation.

"I heard from Amos. He's out there already, waiting for the land to open. As soon as the president declares the unassigned Indian lands open, he will go and get himself a claim."

"Ah, the *Dawes Act*."

"The what?" asked Elizabeth.

"The *Dawes Act*, or *General Allotment Act* that Congress did in 1887 declared that Indian Territory land would not be assigned to tribes, but to individual Indians," Emma said.

"What does that have to do with what we're doing?" asked Jessie, sipping her tea. She had pulled a worn quilt off of Emma's rocker and wrapped herself in it. The fire flickered in the fireplace in front of them, casting a cozy glow around the room.

"Jessie, don't you read the paper?"

"Not much." Jessie laughed. She pulled out a pouch, pinched a wad of tobacco, and shoved it into her cheek.

"You're still doing that vulgar habit?" Emma's eyes shot daggers at Jessie.

"Yep." Jessie chawed. Elizabeth giggled. She had gotten used to Jessie's chaw, but most people were shocked by it.

"Well, since Indian lands are not assigned to tribes anymore, there is some left over. That's what David Payne, the infamous 'Boomer' worked for. To get Indian Territory land opened for white settlers. Seems a little unfair to me."

"Why?" asked Elizabeth.

"White people took all the land up in the West already, why should we take Indian Territory also?"

"Emma, you sure always did think too much."

"And you, never enough," Emma said. Elizabeth laughed again and hiccupped. She swallowed her tea, the warmness sinking all the way to her toes. Next thing she knew, she was jerking awake.

"You two need to get to bed." Emma moved to ready their sleeping arrangements. As she started to walk into the small and only bedroom, Jessie's words stopped her.

"Emma, you got to come with us!" Jessie jumped out the rocker, the quilt falling to the well-polished wood floor.

"Me! Why would I leave my nice home?"

"What have you got holding you here? Your children are grown and moved off. Your husband, God rest his soul, passed on. Come with us!"

Elizabeth nodded off again. Emma said, "Come on, Elizabeth, let's get you to bed." Jessie continued to bother Emma about coming with them.

A week later, scarcely believing it herself, Emma had joined Jessie and Elizabeth. Emma had loudly protested, but in the end, had given in to her older sister's begging. A neighbor had bought her house for his son and she saw nothing holding her back. Emma packed her supply of blankets, quilts, and some foodstuff. They used the money from the sale of the house to buy a Conestoga wagon, horses, and the supplies they needed for the trip.

* * *

Emma's strong hug brought Elizabeth back to the present and she once again asked her, "Why do such awful things have to happen?" Elizabeth's reminiscing had kept her from noticing that Jared had sat down next to her.

Emma began, "Lizzie, God allows bad to happen because he allows humans the ability to choose right and wrong. If he didn't allow choice, we couldn't choose anything for ourselves."

"That doesn't make sense."

Jared said, "I have been thinking about God lately. I blamed him for taking my ma and pa, but now I see it was just evil men, full of hatred that took them. Finding Aenohe helped me to see that."

"But God could have stopped the Indians from killing your parents! God could have stopped the soldiers from killing Aenohe's grandmother! And he didn't!" Elizabeth wrapped her arms around her belly, wondering if God would take this child away from her before she could hold her or him.

"But God doesn't choose to do that all the time, Lizzie, but he chooses to be with us when the bad does happen." Emma wiped a tear from Elizabeth's eye.

"He didn't choose to be with me that night I needed him the most!" Elizabeth said. Jared, next to her, leaned forward, putting his hand on her shoulder.

"How do you know that, Elizabeth?" Jared asked.

"Because he let this happen to me!" She looked down at her abdomen. His eyes held many questions, but they remained inside his head.

Emma began, "Oh, but Elizabeth, God was with you! He led you to Jessie, your friend and cook in your own house, to Nashville to my house, and finally here. He gave you friends who have helped you this far and will continue to help. When times were the roughest, he carried you through." Sam had entered the circle. Elizabeth could not believe she was telling so much of herself to all these people. Sam knelt down.

"I blamed God for taking my Sally, Mrs. Duncan." Sam held his hat in his hands, swallowing hard, Adam's apple moving. He reminded Elizabeth of that day when he had proposed to her. "But I know now that God can bring something good out of bad. It weren't God's fault Sally got a little touched in the head. Mayhap God took her before she hurt herself more."

"But maybe he was just punishing me!" Elizabeth sobbed.

Emma held her. Jared patted her back. Emma prayed aloud, "God comfort this poor hurting soul, let her know you're her God and you love her. Let her know your forgiveness."

Elizabeth sobbed. She soaked the shoulder of Emma's dress but somehow drew comfort from the older woman. She felt a hand pat her back. When she opened her tear-drenched eyes, she saw it was Jared's hand.

# 12

# *Planning*

"What are we going to do with Aenohe?" This phrase became the theme of the next few days. Jared had said they were nearing Purcell and that Judge Parker had warned it would be overflowing with wild people waiting for the lands to open. How could they take Aenohe into that town? He was now a full-fledged member of their ragtag "family." He refused to wear anything but his own "Indian" clothing, but otherwise cooperated.

Sitting by the campfire that evening, Elizabeth and Jared decided it was time they talked to the boy about his future.

"How old are you, son?" asked Jared.

"I do not know. Maybe 14."

"Did you know that you can file for your own land?" asked Elizabeth. "Jared says the Dawes Act made provision for individual Indians, even under-aged ones."

"Grandma didn't want the government handouts."

"But you don't have your grandmother anymore," Jared said gently.

Aenohe hung his head and brushed a tear from his eye. "I just don't know what to do now that she is gone."

Jared looked at Elizabeth. "We have a plan, but you will have to do what we say to make it work."

Aenohe sat, wide-eyed, his brown eyes reflecting the firelight.

Jared began, "You could stay with us, but you will have to cut your hair and dress like we do. We will pass you off as one of us."

"With my dark skin?"

"We could make it work." Elizabeth pleaded with him.

"Or we could go to El Reno after we file our claims and try to get you your own allotment, but I can't promise the soldiers won't just make you go to boarding school," Jared said.

Aenohe simply stared into the distance. Elizabeth's heart went out to him. He had lost everything, just as she had. But this group of friends could help him as they helped her if he would allow it.

"You will be my tribe," Aenohe said. "The world has changed. There is nowhere for me to go. Tomorrow you will cut my hair."

Jared put out his hand and Aenohe grasped it. He walked away and lay down on his bedroll. Elizabeth was so proud of Jared. Aenohe would stay with all of them, as a brother.

The next morning, Elizabeth tried to get in a reading lesson with Jared before they hit the trail. Jeremiah and Doc kept their distance as she got out a slate, they had finally purchased. Jared had this one curl right in front that hung over his eyes. He had a line around his head where his hat sat. It made her smile.

"I guess these hands were made for holding reins not pencils." He shrugged as he looked at his attempt at copying her straight letters.

"You did well, Jared."

"You're just saying that to make me feel good."

"I think you know I wouldn't do that."

"I don't know you well at all, Lizzie." The sound of her shortened name on his breath made her heart pound.

She looked at her hands.

"What don't you know that you want to know?"

"I suppose all those things I wonder wouldn't be polite to ask, now would they?" He stared at her protruding waistline.

"You want to know about the baby's father." She placed her hand on her belly.

"Did you love him?"

"I thought I did."

"But he's dead now?"

She closed her mouth and clenched her jaw. *Could she trust him? He had seemed so trustworthy. But then, so had William. How could she tell him what had really happened? How could she tell him that William had hurt her in so many ways including physically? How could she say that she didn't know whether he was alive or dead and did not care? Or did she? Did she love him still? How had she loved such a man?*

"Jared, I'm just not ready to talk about it."

"Elizabeth, when you are, I'm here." He took her tiny hand in his large, callous one. Despite the calluses, his hand felt gentle as it closed around hers in a soft squeeze. She had been trained to believe that no touching between a man and woman was acceptable until engagement, even marriage, but she knew this was not inappropriate. Jared offered his friendship to her.

She dared look in his eyes. What did she see there? Compassion. She did not see pity. She saw the eyes of a friend.

She sought to change the subject. "Do you think we will get trouble over Aenohe in Purcell?"

Jared took a deep breath and let it out slowly. "Elizabeth, the land allotted to his tribe is about 80 miles west of here. As an Indian child, he is entitled to a section of his own."

"But he says he doesn't want it."

"I want him to stay with us for now. After I get my own land, I'll take him to the authorities and have his land assigned to him if he changes his mind. If not, he can help me work my land. "

"But, Jared, what if the soldiers shoot him? Or make him go to a boarding school?"

"I won't let that happen."

"You will go against the United States government?"

"I don't know, Elizabeth. I just don't know."

"Move out!" They heard Jeremiah's voice boom out. Jared doused the fire and Elizabeth took her place on the wagon seat next to Jessie as Jared mounted his horse. "Purcell here we come."

*Part Four*

# *Oklahoma Territory*

March–April 1889

# 13

## *The Town*

IN PURCELL, OKLAHOMA TERRITORY, one mentality prevailed: "Get land!" No one talked about anything else. Just yesterday President Benjamin Harrison had signed the proclamation that the land would be opened on April 22. The land would open with a horse race! Everyone would line up on horseback, with their wagon, on foot, or take the train, and the first person to register each homestead would receive it. Today was March 24. Counting down the hours to April 22 was the favorite pastime.

They made camp on the south side of the city. Tents stretched as far as the eye could see.

"I'm going to skedaddle into the center of town to see what I can learn." Jared hollered as galloped by on his Palomino.

"I'm coming with you." Sam LeBeau stepped into his saddle as he called.

*Leaving the women to set up camp as usual*, Elizabeth thought. Her protruding abdomen made bending over almost impossible. Jessie made their camp and shushed Elizabeth when she tried to help. Aenohe stayed with the women. Elizabeth knew he feared someone recognizing his heritage even though Jared had cut his hair and given him his only other set of clothing. Jared promised to buy Aenohe a hat as he galloped away.

"There's one time in a woman's life when she's allowed to be idle, and you're going to take it!"

Most women heard that from their husbands. Elizabeth did not have a husband to say those things. She thought of William. . . *no*, she told herself, *I won't think of William.* Her thoughts turned to Jared.

"I've got to find Amos." Jessie fretted as she started a fire.

"Just go, Jessie! I'm sure some saloon character will know where to find him. You know how men are about those things. They say women gossip!" Elizabeth fanned her face. The exertion to make camp had made her sweat in spite of the fifty-degree weather.

"After supper."

Doc Sims swaggered by as they began cooking. *He's probably looking for a handout,* Elizabeth thought. Jessie ignored the hint of the doctor. Elizabeth thought perhaps Jessie was through with him. She hoped so. The more she got to know him, the more she wished she hadn't.

"Emma, you just get over here and eat with us." Jessie turned around to see Emma attempting to start a fire.

"A welcome invitation. I've got cornbread left from lunch."

Jessie offered, wad-in-cheek, "That'll go fine with the beans we've had stewing."

The children tagged after her, Jenny's nose running as usual. Elizabeth wiped it with the edge of her apron. Jenny flashed her dimpled smile.

"We womenfolk gotta stick together, you know," Jessie remarked. Out of the corner of her eye, she shot daggers at the doc. He sat munching a sandwich, attempting to ignore her. Jeremiah Brown jumped out of his wagon. Dressed in a brown suit, he looked ready to face anything. Aenohe backed away from Jeremiah in fear. Jeremiah ignored him.

"Well, ladies, wish me luck! I'm off to make my fortune."

"Gambling?" Jessie asked tactlessly.

"My business." He saddled his horse, mounted, and rode away.

Jessie washed the supper dishes. Daylight faded into twilight. She announced she was walking to town to look for Amos. Emma turned to ready the children for bed.

"But Ma, we want to stay up!" Elizabeth noted they were already calling her Ma after such a short time. *Good for them*, she thought. *If only Aunt Jane had opened her heart to me in that way. . .*

*Elizabeth, you've got to realize you're only an orphan. We took you in. You owe us very much. You must be nice to us. You've got to be grateful.* Her aunt's words raced across her mind. Never once had she held her as Emma hugged her stepchildren every day.

Elizabeth readied herself for bed, wondering why she even bothered. Lately, she had not been able to get more sleep than half an hour at a time. The constant pressure on her bladder made her exceptionally miserable. Especially where they were camped, for there were no comforts of any privies around, she and Jessie had a chamber pot in the wagon that they emptied when they could. The stench of the urine usually drove Elizabeth to empty it right away and lugging it in and out of the wagon made her wish for a diaper like the ones she had fashioned out of scrap flannel for the baby.

Finally, after turning from side to side for an hour, she settled into a fitful slumber. Sometime in the night, between privy breaks, Jessie sneaked into her bedroll next to Elizabeth. The soft snoring against her back in the close quarters brought comfort to Elizabeth. More than once she had thought of Jessie as the mother she never had. What would she have done without her?

When the baby kicked, Elizabeth awakened to the signs of dawn drawing their way across the sky. She decided to stay up this time. Jessie rolled over, a muffled snore causing Elizabeth to giggle. She stepped out of the wagon and saw Jared at his fire.

"Morning."

"Morning."

"So, what news do you have to share this morning?" She teased as she waddled over to talk to him.

"News?" His look was too innocent.

"Well, what did you find out?"

"About what?"

"Jared, are you going to sneak into the territory early like those other Sooners?"

"Well, I met some that are setting out this morning to look for a claim."

"But obviously you're not with them."

"No, Elizabeth, I found out what the penalty is if you get caught. You can never file a claim in Oklahoma Territory."

"Well, I never thought something like that would deter a cowboy like you. You're used to risks. You can surely avoid a few federal agents."

"I talked to a few who had heard about what happened to some Sooners."

"And. . .?"

"Federal agents shot them. No questions asked. One of the men was unarmed."

"Why, that's just plain murder, Jared." Elizabeth lowered herself to the saddle delete return next to Jared's fire, next to Aenohe who ate silently.

"Yeah, well, there's so much corruption going on that the federal agents want the land to themselves. If you had asked me to take this risk two years ago I'd have done it. But after risking everything with my cattle venture, I'm not as dumb as I once was."

"Maybe you're just not as young."

"That's mighty smart words coming from one so young."

"Why, Jared, you know it's impolite to refer to a lady's age." She grinned.

"Lady? Why I guess you to be 18 or 19!"

"Hmmph." She got up and stomped to her own fire with all the dignity of her eighteen years. She knew she was just reinforcing his knowledge of her age by acting like a child, but she could not bear to be laughed at for being young.

"Elizabeth. . ." He followed her.

Just then Emma's brood bounded from their white canvas tent. The screaming and chasing that accompanied little ones made continuing their conversation impossible. Jessie woke up yelling at the children to shut their mouths. Jessie hollered at Sam to "Shut his young'uns up" and Sam shouted back for Jessie to mind her own business. This was such a typical morning. Elizabeth laughed to herself. She smiled at Jared to let him know she was not mad. She had acted younger than little Jenny.

"Jessie, did you find him?" Elizabeth asked as they settled down to a cold corn muffin breakfast. Jessie sipped her coffee. The doctor had emerged from his tent looking like he had drunk the saloon dry the previous evening. Jessie's eyes darted to his and turned back to her coffee.

"What? Oh, no, I didn't find him. But I found a fellow who said he might be able to locate him for a tidy sum of money."

"Well?"

"I figure I don't need to hire some cowboy to find my own son. I reckon I'll just ask some more folks today."

"I've been thinking, Jessie. We should get jobs while we're here. We'll be here for a month."

"Good idea. What could we do?"

"We passed a store on the way that had an ad in the window for a seamstress. I learned to sew at Mrs. Rind's School for Girls. I don't see many other women around, do you? Maybe we could both do it."

"I don't relish the idea of being holed up in some fancy–pants store working for an old man." A stream of tobacco left her mouth at full force. If Elizabeth had not been used to it, she would have jumped back. But Jessie never hit her. Her aim, as usual, was accurate.

"Well, what do you intend on doing?"

Jessie shot another dagger at the doctor. "Don't know yet."

"Why don't you take in laundry? Women's work is good for you." The doc put his two–cent remark into the conversation.

"Elizabeth, did you hear something? I thought I heard a fly buzzing next to my ear, or maybe a mosquito." Jessie turned her back, ignoring him.

"You two are on your way to driving me insane!" Elizabeth voiced in frustration, throwing up her arms. "You are worse than Jenny and Johnny!"

"I'm on my way to find my son. Excuse me!" Jessie slammed her tin coffee cup down and pushed to her feet. She stomped off towards town again.

"Jessie, wait! I want to come with you! You can't leave me here all day!" Elizabeth shouted.

"I don't need a parson preaching at me!" Jessie continued on her way.

"And here I was going to offer her a ride on my horse." Doc Sims commented.

"Shut up!" Elizabeth threw the dishwater on the fire. She reached under the wagon canvas to grab her threadbare bonnet.

Elizabeth decided she would walk to town herself and apply for a job, but wondered if she should leave Aenohe alone. The impropriety of the matter crossed her mind. She mentally ticked off the list of "Nice Girls Don't-Do's" in her head. Nice girls never walk to town without a chaperon. Nice girls never need to work for a living. And most of all, nice girls never, never allow themselves to be seen in public while in the family way. *Well, Aunt Jane, sometimes nice girls don't have a choice.*

She had no money and planned to take this opportunity to earn something. She washed her hands and face. Smoothing the wrinkles on her one clean dress, she wanted to despair. *Who in their right mind would hire a hugely pregnant woman?* Back home, Elizabeth had never even seen anyone this advanced in their pregnancy. *What a sheltered life I led. But one thing about living with Jessie has taught me. Grip life by the horns and change things yourself.* Sitting around feeling sorry for oneself never did anything. Nothing stopped Jessie from looking for her one remaining son anyway.

She heard hoofbeats. Jared. She poked her head out of the canvas flap.

"Jared, I must go into town."

"Why?"

"I need a job. I have no money."

His eyes ran over her distended figure. She saw the look in his eye. Of course, pregnant women were not supposed to work.

"I know! I know! But what else am I supposed to do?"

"I guess you can't sit on this horse with me. Let me hitch up your wagon. I'll go with you. This town ain't fit for woman or child." He chuckled at his little joke. He handed Aenohe a hat, saying, "Here, son, this might keep some eyes off you."

"Thanks," said Aenohe.

"Stay here and watch the camp, Aenohe, and stay out of sight if you see any soldiers."

"I will."

As they drove away a few minutes later, Elizabeth heard Emma singing a hymn as she hung the laundry to dry.

"Marriage sure seems to have done that woman good," Jared remarked.

"Yes, they sure seem to be happy."

"Yeah."

"Emma credits the Lord for her joy. She doesn't give Sam *all* the credit." Elizabeth said.

"Wonder why the Almighty don't make everyone that happy?"

"Jared, I don't understand it myself. I'm a Christian. I was raised in the church, baptized and confirmed. I never missed a Sunday."

"Some folks take their religion more serious than others I reckon."

They pulled on to the main street of Purcell. Not even in the cities back east had Elizabeth ever seen so many people crammed into such a small space. Loud noises came from everywhere. Gunshots, screaming, and piano music filled the dusty air. Yet Elizabeth's eyes could not pick out a saloon.

"Where are the saloons, Jared?"

"They're in the river." He pointed down the hill that was Main Street. "The river is down there."

"Why?"

Jared explained patiently. "Purcell is in Indian Territory. Lexington, the town to the west, is in Oklahoma Territory. Understand so far?"

"I thought it was all Indian Territory."

"A common mistake."

"The government won't allow liquor to be sold in Indian Territory, but it's legal in Oklahoma Territory. Lexington is full of saloons."

"But you said Purcell's saloons were in the river?" Elizabeth asked.

The men of the town have built several saloons on flat bottom boats in the river. That way they ain't in Indian Territory, but the Lexington men don't get all the money."

"I think Jeremiah and Doc both headed to one."

Silence.

Elizabeth could tell Jared wouldn't discuss Jeremiah. *Is he jealous?* She wondered.

"I want to see those saloons."

"Elizabeth!"

"Just from the riverbank!"

"Well, if you insist. Let's drive to the end of Main Street, and I'll point them out to you." The wagon moved down a steep hill. Jared had to pull on the reigns to slow them down. At the bottom of the hill, the river churned, red and muddy in its swollen spring state. She saw what looked like a few shacks floating in the river.

"Those are saloons?"

"Yeah, look at that one. It has two stories. One for drinking and gambling, and one for–" He stopped suddenly, realizing he was in the presence of a lady.

"I know. You don't have to say it." A sick feeling in the pit of her stomach rose to her throat. What if Jared knew the truth about her?

Jared pulled back on the reigns once more so he could turn the horses. They pulled the wagon back up the hill to the shops. Elizabeth saw a sign that said

CAMP MEETING TONIGHT IN BRUSH ARBOR
EAST OF CITY.
COME HEAR THE LORD'S MESSAGE AND SOME
GOOD SINGING.

"You ever been to a revival meeting, Jared?"

"Yeah, my parents dragged me to a few in Kansas. Those Methodist preachers sure got riled up. Me and my brothers used to sit in the back row and laugh at the old fellows."

"I went to a few at church, but nothing outside. It might be interesting."

"Is that a hint? You want me to take you?"

"No, if I want to go, I'll go myself."

"I been thinking, Elizabeth. . . as independent as you are, you ought to get yourself hooked up with those suffragettes. You know, the ones who think women should vote."

"Jared, you constantly surprise me. I've never heard a man actually encourage a woman to do that."

Just then they arrived at the store Elizabeth remembered. Since the help wanted sign still in the window, she accepted Jared's help out of the wagon.

"Morning. May I help you?" The handle–bar mustached gentleman behind the counter stared at her. "I'd like to apply for the position of seamstress." Elizabeth looked him square in the eye.

"Mister, you allow your wife to work in her uh–condition?"

"She's not my wife. She's a friend, and a widow. I expect you to speak to her about the position, not me." Jared turned and walked out the door. Elizabeth did not know whether to be thankful or furious at him for leaving her to defend herself.

"Well, now, hmm. . . do you have a sample of your sewing?"

"No, but I can bring one to you."

"Well, I hate to hire someone in your condition, but since no one else has applied for the position, I'll offer it to you on a trial basis. Bring a sample of your work in the morning at eight and be prepared to work until six in the evening." She guessed she could bring a baby dress she had sewn. "What about my wages?"

"Twenty–five cents a shirt and fifty cents a dress."

She signed and agreed, putting out her hand so they could shake on it.

Elizabeth lumbered out of the store and into the dusty street, wondering how she would stand working in such a crowded little shop. She took a deep breath. The baby kicked its protest.

"Well?" Jared stood next to the horses.

"He offered it to me on a trial basis."

Crash! The window of the hotel next to the dry goods store crumbled to pieces. A chair flew out the hole and hit the horse. They reared and bolted. Jared jumped back out of the way just in time. He bumped into Elizabeth. He had to put his arms around her to steady himself. In the flash of a moment, she smelled the scent of the soap on his newly clean-shaven face. He pushed away and hastened down the street shouting, "Whoa!"

Elizabeth wondered if anything else could go wrong on this long journey. Her back ached, her nose itched, her eyes watered from the dust. And now she had lost Jessie's horses. She thought longingly of the hotel in Fort Smith and wished someone knew someone here. She wished for a nice, soft bed and clean clothes. Instead, she plopped herself on a bench to wait for Jared to come back.

People passed her. One phrase kept floating to her ears. "Harrison signed the bill." She wondered wryly if President Harrison had any idea what he had done to this town.

Few women walked in the streets. The properly chaperoned ladies threw her the disapproving looks that she herself would have given a woman like her only a few months ago. Dressed in their plumed hats placed on curled hair, ruffled skirts swishing over four or five petticoats, they made her feel filthy and trashy. Her one petticoat hung in rags under her watermelon-sized belly. She determined that she would buy some material for a new petticoat with her earnings.

She stood to stretch her cramped legs. Gratefully, she saw Jared trekking down the way with Jessie's horses in tow, their sides lathered.

"How'd you catch them?"

"Some nice fellow a ways up the road caught them for me."

"I hope they didn't hurt anyone."

"Nope. People have learned to jump out of the way. Guess this happens a lot around here."

As they inched their way through the crowds back to their camp, Elizabeth asked, "Jared, will Guthrie be this way?"

"Be what way?"

"A den of iniquity, as my aunt would say."

"Probably."

"I guess when you started talking to me about a new city, I was naïve enough to imagine one like Alexandria."

"Well, eventually it will be. That's why they need proper ladies like you. To calm the place down and make it civilized."

"Jared, I'm not proper anymore. I keep company with a man with no escort. I have a job. I'm in the family way out in public every day. I might as well be a mill–worker's wife."

"Well, now, Elizabeth, I hoped that aunt of yours taught you that being a lady is a state of mind. Like being a westerner, or a cowboy. I'll always be a westerner even if I hang up my hat and live in town one day. Do you understand?"

"I guess. I'm just so ashamed of what I've become."

"And the alternative is. . ."

"To crawl back to Virginia and marry. . ." She clamped her head over her mouth. She had almost let it slip.

"What?"

"Oh nothing. I just don't want the alternative." They had arrived at their camp. Jared helped her off the wagon. She watched him jump down and begin unhitching. No sign of Jessie, the Doc, or Jeremiah. Emma lay in the shade of the wagon while the children played.

During supper, Elizabeth talked to Jessie about the Camp Meeting. Jessie did not sound a bit interested. Emma said that she would go, but she did not think she had the strength or the energy. Elizabeth determined she would go herself. As she expressed her disgust at all of their lack of interest in spiritual things, Jared walked up behind her.

"I'll take you."

She whirled around. "Why thank you. Let me freshen up."

They sat in the wagon again, taking the well–worn path to town. At the end of the main street, they headed east. Soon they saw a brush arbor, and many wagons pulled around it. Elizabeth could hear the noise of a cheap pump organ.

Jared helped Elizabeth down over the wagon. She was glad she had on the dress she had bought with Jeremiah's money. It was at least in one piece and did not strain around her belly. Jared held his head high, as if he were escorting a real lady, and not a low–life pregnant woman. But then, he thought she was a lady. She had left her right to be a lady behind in Virginia just as she had left all her fancy dresses.

They took a place on a hard makeshift bench. People filled in the benches around them. Elizabeth noted quite a few snotty-nosed children and a few equally filthy mothers. Mixed in the crowd were also people dressed in the finery she had seen in her aunt's crowd at home.

"Are you comfortable?" Jared whispered. *Comfortable?* She had not been comfortable in three months!

"Yes," she lied, pulling the quilt around her she had brought in lieu of a shawl.

Just then a short, round little man in with chops and a mustache stood up in the front of the arbor. He started singing an old hymn and soon everyone joined in. They sang and sang. Elizabeth sang the old hymns she had learned in church as a child, but had never heard them sung with such fervor. When they got to *Amazing Grace*, even Jared joined.

The round little song leader sat down. A tall, balding, rather thin man of perhaps forty stood up behind the makeshift pulpit. He began to preach, but Elizabeth had never heard preaching like this. His point was thus, "There will be a judgment one day and we will all stand before God. Some will go to heaven and some to hell!" The way he described hell made Elizabeth smell the fire. She fidgeted. Out of the corner of her eye, she noted Jared. He remained expressionless. She did not want to go to hell. Of course, she could not go to hell. She had been baptized as a child. She was a Christian. Then why was she scared?

As they drove back to camp, Jared asked her what she thought of the meeting.

"The singing was wonderful."

"Yeah. I liked it."

"But the preaching. . ." she did not quite know what to say.

"Like a lot of preaching I heard before."

"I've never heard anything like it."

"Seems to me that if folks want to join up with God, they don't need the hell scared out of 'em," Jared said.

"Are you criticizing the preacher?"

"Yeah. Why not?"

"We didn't dare do that at home."

"You afraid God will strike you dead if you do?" He smiled.

"No."

"Elizabeth, what's wrong?"

"I'm just afraid of hell, I guess."

"Oh, come on! Don't let that loud, arrogant lunatic get to you!"

They remained silent until they returned to camp. Elizabeth fretted and bit her nails. She wondered if she could ever forget about the hellfire.

# 14

## *Jessie's Plan*

LOOKING UP FROM THE calico shirt she was basting, she saw Jessie walk into the dressmakers' shop. Elizabeth's jaw dropped almost to the floor.

"Jessie!" Elizabeth put the shirt down and stood to behold the transformed woman in front of her. Jessie had traded her threadbare calico dress for a red and white checkered shirt tucked into an ugly pair of men's trousers. A leather belt filled with bullets wrapped around her thin waist, at which on her right side was attached a holster with a shiny new gun inside it.

"Aren't you afraid of getting arrested for wearing those trousers?" asked Elizabeth. "And what about the gun? Where did you get it?"

"I bought this gun back in Tennessee, don't you remember?" Jessie fingered the shiny metal as she pulled the gun from her hip. "By the way, I sold the wagon and stored our stuff, except for this bag of clothes." She set their old carpetbag down.

"What's with the gun?"

"Heard tell claim jumpers are everywhere. Have to defend my claim, now won't I?"

"Jessie, you are truly serious about this aren't you? "

"Serious as I'll ever be about anything. What am I supposed to do, sit around? I'm used to farming. Done my share on your uncle's farm for years. I want land to call my own. When that gun sounds in two days I will be racing for my life"

"I guess you will." Elizabeth laughed. She had just looked down at Jessie's pointed-toe leather boots.

"Spurs! Jessie you've got to be kidding!"

"I plan on making that horse move, Elizabeth!" A twinkle in her eye made Elizabeth sit down she was laughing so hard. Jessie reached down and pulled her heel up to twirl the shiny metal like a windmill blowing in the endless Oklahoma wind.

"Excuse me, did I hear someone mention riding in this run?" A woman in a red sunbonnet walked nearer to Elizabeth and Jessie.

"Yes, I am." Jessie's look dared the woman to challenge her.

"Well, ain't that a fact."

"You got something to say, now, say it."

"I've got an easier way for you to get land." She handed Jessie a crumpled piece of paper and walked, no, marched out the door.

Just then Mr. Rand came into the shop. He looked at Elizabeth and gave her a glance that said she had better get back to work.

"I'll see you at camp, Jessie."

Jessie shoved the paper in her pocket and walked back into the noisy, dusty street.

Later, Elizabeth sat at their make-shift camp. Jessie came riding up *astride* Elizabeth noted wryly.

"Elizabeth!" Jessie yelled.

Elizabeth waited. Jessie had been so loud lately. She shoved the crumpled paper under Elizabeth's nose.

> WOMEN'S MEETING
> IF YOU'RE INTERESTED IN GETTING LAND
> MEET AT THE CHURCH ON FIRST STREET
> TONIGHT AT SUNDOWN

"Sounds like a scam." Jared looked over their shoulders. "There's a scam for every person in this town! Why I just heard yesterday someone was selling lots in a town that don't exist!"

"You're just jealous because men weren't invited!" Jessie jabbed.

"Suit yourself." Jared walked away shaking his head and muttering under his breath, "Women. . ."

"Are you going?"

"Of course. Might as well. Maybe this woman knows something I don't."

"You've got to let me come too, then I won't have you going alone."

"Did I just hear you order me around?"

"Jessie!"

"You can come."

"I wasn't asking permission!"

Elizabeth wondered suddenly where they would sleep tonight now that Jessie had sold her wagon. "So, Jessie, what do you plan to do about sleeping accommodations now that you sold our moving house?"

"Sleeping what?" Jessie spit a coffee-colored stream to the ground.

"Where are we going to sleep tonight?"

"Got us hotel rooms."

"But every hotel room in this town has been full for months."

"I had me some connections."

Once again Elizabeth was aghast at Jessie's antics. But she was too grateful at the thought of a soft bed to question whether Jessie had obtained the rooms in an honest way.

"What about the others?"

"They're going to keep their wagons and stay here. You and Emma can ride the Boomer train to the land openings."

Doc sauntered up to them. "Hey, Jessie, where's your wagon?"

"Sold it." She turned her back to him.

"Wow, Jessie. Trousers. Spurs. You must be about to become a cowboy."

"Shut up, Doc, you wouldn't know a cowboy if it roped your neck."

"Ain't nothing sweeter than a sassy woman."

Elizabeth saw Jessie's hackles rise. Jessie walked over to the Doc. Elizabeth felt sure Jessie would slap the smirk right off his face. Instead, she marched within an inch of his body, and said, "You, Doc Sims, are the orneriest, ugliest, meanest, most yeller–livered sorry excuse for a man that ever set foot on American soil. I regret any associations I had with you in the past. You are a skunk."

"Jessie, are you still riled up over that Indian boy?"

"He is not an 'Indian boy.' His name is Aenohe and he is a part of this group now."

"You're adorable when you're mad."

She stomped away. Elizabeth tried to stifle a giggle. Then asked, "Where is our carpetbag?"

"In Emma's wagon. She's going to drive us to the hotel."

"What did you do, Jessie?"

"It was only a few coins for the rooms. Just for a couple nights."

They walked to the shabby excuse for a hotel later that evening. The skinny clerk showed them to their room. Jessie and Elizabeth shared a room that Elizabeth could not believe was not called a closet. The bed looked wrinkled and dirty. The floor was filthy, and the furniture worn. She thought with longing of the luxurious room they had left in Fort Smith. *Oh well*, she sighed. *This cannot be worse than the wagon or a tent.*

Jessie began removing her trousers. Elizabeth turned her head. She could hear Aunt Jane remarking about a woman they had seen in trousers once. The judgment had been so severe that Elizabeth would not even allow the words to cross her mind. Yet she knew those things were not true about Jessie. *Did a lady have to wear a dress?* She wondered. *What is wrong with dressing comfortably? Is it really a sin?* Jessie broke all the rules that Elizabeth had been taught to follow as a girl. But she was still a lady at heart, and with that, a heart of gold.

They settled down for the night. Elizabeth could not sleep as usual; the baby wedged its foot against her ribs and brought extreme discomfort. She didn't move because she did not want to disturb Jessie. Instead, she tried to think of what she would teach this child if it were a girl. Would she train her in the ways she had been trained? How could she? She did not believe in those things herself. Even so, she did not want the girl to go through the hardships she had gone through.

Flashbacks made her catch her breath. It was the night Aunt Jane had discovered Elizabeth's pregnancy.

*She had walked in the room while Elizabeth was undressing. She saw her belly, the belly that Elizabeth had tried so hard to hide in the new empire waist style of dress. A look that could only be described as extreme shock crossed her face—"Elizabeth Louise Lee!"*

*Elizabeth turned. She looked at her feet. "Yes."*

*"You are in the family way."*

*"Yes."*

*"You hussy! You are no better than your whoring mother!" Aunt Jane raised the back of her hand and slapped her face. Elizabeth raised her hand to the spot. Aunt Jane rarely hit her.*

*"But—it wasn't—my—fault." She tried to speak.*

*"What do you mean it wasn't your fault?"*

*"William—he—"*

*"He forced you?"*

*"Yes, he was drunk at the time. He overpowered me."*

*"You expect me to believe that after you chased after that man?"*

*"Aunt Jane, you wanted me to chase him! You told me to make sure I was set for life with a rich man!"*

*Another slap. "How dare you blame me for this!" Elizabeth grew silent.*

*"Listen to me, girl, you will marry that man. No one will have you now. It's his child, he will take responsibility."*

*"I won't!"*

An exceptionally strong kick brought Elizabeth back to the stuffy hotel room. She wished she could blot out all of those memories. What she would give for happiness again. She thought of her conversation with Emma about God's love and forgiveness and grace. She wondered if she believed it. The preacher back home had always said God had reserved hell for people like her, and so had the preacher at the camp meeting. God could never forgive her.

# 15

## *Speculating*

FOR THE NEXT THREE weeks, Elizabeth sewed shirts and dresses in the stuffy little dress shop. Afterward, Jared, Jessie, Sam, or Emma would pick her up in a wagon and they would eat. Then Elizabeth and Jessie would try to sleep in their noisy, stuffy hotel room. Jeremiah and Doc stayed busy gambling on the boats; Elizabeth saw them occasionally. Sam had managed to get a job hauling for a store and made a few dollars here and there.

Jessie's whereabouts during the day were a mystery. Finally, one evening, she invited Elizabeth to a meeting.

"What kind of meeting, Jessie?" I'm tired, and I don't want to hear any more preachers screaming at me about hellfire."

"You know I don't go to church, girl, this is a women's meeting."

"You mean about voting? You'd think the women would have enough to worry about right now."

Jessie stuck a new plug of tobacco in her mouth. "Na, it's not about voting. It's about forming a town."

"You mean a town like Guthrie? I thought we'd already agreed we were going there." Elizabeth brushed at her thick curls as Jessie sat on the rickety bed across from her.

"No, girl, this is a town of all women. No men allowed."

Elizabeth laughed. "Who ever heard of such a thing, Jessie? And why would you want to live without men? Some of them aren't so bad." She thought of Jared, waiting for her outside.

"Aren't you tired of Doc and Jeremiah and their stinky habits? And what about William?" Jessie stood, with her hands on her hips.

Elizabeth bristled. "Jessie, you know I asked you never to mention him!"

"See, you hate men as much as I do, or are you getting sweet on Jared?"

"I'm not sweet on anyone, Jessie! He's my friend, and he's a good man! I don't approve of their gambling, drinking, smoking and cussing, but Doc and Jeremiah have *some* good qualities. We couldn't have made it here without them! Besides, I thought *you* were *sweet* on Doc."

"How can I be sweet on that skunk? Never you mind! I'll go myself." Jessie slammed the door and stomped down the stairs.

Elizabeth laughed and then walked down the stairs herself to meet Jared, Aenohe, Sam, Emma, and the children. They were going to discuss their game plan for the Run as it was only days away. Jessie would have to manage on her own.

"I'm going to board my herd and wagon here and return for them after I get my claim." Jared said as they all sat around a fire outside of town later that night.

"Emma, Jenny, Johnny, and Elizabeth can take the train from here to Guthrie, and we can meet them there," Sam said.

"I'm not sure I like the idea of getting separated, Sam." Emma's gentle voice interrupted the masculine planning.

"There's no other way, Honey, it'll be too dangerous out there trying to get a claim."

"I don't think it's going to be much better on the train," remarked Elizabeth, "This entire town is in a frenzy that will just escalate by the twenty–second."

"Jared is going to ride his horse. I'm going to take my wagon. I can't afford to leave it here." Sam spoke as if he had made up his mind. He glanced at Aenohe, who lay sleeping on a blanket.

"Anyone heard from Doc or Jeremiah?" asked Elizabeth.

Jared and Sam looked at each other.

"What?"

"I heard they may be trying other ways to get land," said Jared, shrugging his shoulders.

"You mean they've connected with some Sooners?" asked Emma.

"That's the rumor down at the riverboats," said Sam.

"What were you doing down in that den of iniquity?" Emma's hackles rose.

"Honey, it is the only place to get real news around here. The papers can't keep up with the steady stream of changes to the rumors!" Sam grasped his hat and moved it round and round as he often did when nervous.

"What about Jessie?" Jared looked at Elizabeth for the answer.

"Even I can't predict Jessie's moods these days, Jared. If she plans on riding the train with us, I don't know. When Emma and I bought tickets yesterday she didn't want to go with us." A fuss from the wagon brought Emma to her feet, and she disappeared to check on Johnny. Elizabeth bit a nail. She did not want to end this journey without Jessie.

"Tonight, you get her to give you a straight answer, Elizabeth. Speaking of, it's time to get you to your room." Jared stood as Sam doused the fire. He helped Elizabeth to her feet and aided her in climbing to his wagon. Elizabeth hoped Jessie would have returned from her meeting by the time she returned to the room.

"Jared, what about Aenohe? What is he going to do while you and Sam are running for your claims?" Elizabeth's voice was heavy with concern. "We can't take him on the train."

"He's going to ride with Sam in his wagon."

"Oh." Fatigue had claimed every inch of her being, and she was grateful her sewing job had ended that day. No one wanted anything sewn as they were all too busy packing for the Run.

# 16

# *The Boomer Train*

"ALL ABOARD!" THE CONDUCTOR yelled as the Boomer Train headed to Guthrie blew its whistle.

"Well, I guess this is good-bye."

"Yeah, guess so."

"Elizabeth."

"Yes, Jared."

"I'm going straight for the land around Guthrie. Stay in town until Sam and I get there. Stay with Emma. There is no telling what Jessie will do." Jessie had changed her mind at the last minute about riding her horse and tied him to Sam's wagon. She had agreed to ride the train with them, but Elizabeth still did not see her. Her eyes scanned the crowd and saw every race and economic status known to humanity in front of her. Old and young, weak and strong, rich and poor, it was as if the entire country had turned out for this chance at free land. For the first time, she realized not everyone would get what they wanted. *What would happen if they did not get claims?*

"Yes! I'll meet you there." All her apprehension disappeared in the heat of the moment.

"Get READY!" The cry rang out. Jared swung on his horse and raced to the  growing line of horses and wagons.

Emma, the children, and Elizabeth shoved their way into the crowded car at one o'clock. People were still shouting, crazy to get to what was left of the free land. She heard one man say that Oklahoma Station was his stop.

"Give me a window seat!" A man yelled as he squished his way past her. "I'm going to jump when I see an open claim."

"As if there's any left!" An older woman sniffed.

Clutching her carpetbag her close to her side, she thought, *today is a day full of dreams.* She took in sights and smells and feelings that she might tell her baby of the day's events. Surely such an unusual event would be written in history books. No seats were left when she entered her assigned car. People were standing in the aisles. Luckily her condition lent itself to people showing their manners. Three men and four women offered her seats. She took the seat that one of the men offered. Emma squeezed in next to her, the children holding to both of their skirts.

As she leaned back and shut her eyes to close out the crowd, Elizabeth tried to straighten everything out in her mind that Jessie had told her. Claim a townsite in her name. How would she do it? She glanced at Emma's Winchester in its case and laughed inwardly at the thought of an obviously pregnant woman standing guard over a townsite while shouldering a gun.

"Hello, Mrs. Duncan, Mrs. LeBeau." She noticed Doc Sims.

"Hey, Doctor, I thought you were already long gone," said Emma.

"Oh, I have my ways of doing things."

"Great. You must have had some contact with a Sooner or two?" asked Emma.

"Perhaps."

Elizabeth pleaded, "Please, Doc, you have to help me. I want a townsite to open a dress shop. It's my only hope of supporting myself. But I'm underage. Jessie told me to file in her name, but she's already registering for a homestead. I hear they give you trouble over trying to register to two claims."

"Hmm. You sound desperate. Girl, what you need is a man to support you. I'm sure if you batted your eyes at Jeremiah, he'd propose. He's back there on the train somewhere." She ignored that. If only she was not pregnant, she would have run with the rest.

"I'll pay you after I bring in some money, I promise."

"Maybe we could strike a deal. You see, I got my eye on Jessie. You talk her into marrying me and I'll–"

Suddenly someone shouted, "Guthrie!" Doc scrambled to his feet so fast he practically ran over Elizabeth. She despaired that they had never agreed on a deal.

The trains slowed as it chug–chugged into Guthrie station. Elizabeth decided to wait to stand. Her back ached and she thought she would suffocate from the dust. A sharp cramp started in her back and wound its way forward to her middle. She clutched her abdomen and gasped. Emma, across from her, grabbed her arm.

"Child, it's time!"

"No, Emma, it's early! It's just a cramp."

"Whatever it is, we've got to get you some help. Come along, children."

*Not now, baby!* She screamed inwardly.

She took a deep breath. Jessie had described a contraction to her. This fit the description. She would not admit it to Emma. Maybe if she didn't it would all go away.

Ten minutes later she stood and made her way into the crowd moving in one direction. As she stepped off the train, some fashionably dressed women gave her polite but disgusted looks. She looked at their tiny waists in their ruffled gowns with puffed sleeves and wanted to scream. Her aunt's words to her months before ran through her mind, "A lady never allows others to see her in advanced stages of the family way."

*"Well, Aunt Jane, sometimes you don't have a choice,"* she whispered.

Another contraction seized her. This one was even harder. It took her breath away. What could she expect? What kind of mother would squeeze herself into an overcrowded train a month before her baby was due to birth? What kind of a mother expected to have a normal pregnancy after travelling halfway across the continent on foot or in a spring-less prairie schooner?

*What am I going to do?* She looked up and down the make-shift street. Buildings were literally flying upwards; sawdust flew in all directions.

"Emma!" She lost sight of her.

"I'm here!" Emma raised an arm, a smaller hand clasped in hers.

The sound of saws, hammers, nails, and shouts of workmen filled the air. No sign of Jared, Sam, or Jessie. Doc Sims had disappeared into the street filled with tents and raw lumber. Elizabeth crossed the tracks.

"Where's the land office?" That's where I should be heading, she thought.

*If only I could find the doctor!* There was not even anywhere to sit. She walked, not knowing what else to do. Emma finally caught up to her, the children straggling behind. "Come on. Jenny, grab Johnny's hand."

Emma held Elizabeth's hand. The road, or rather, field, in front of them went uphill.

"Can you make it up this hill?"

"I–hhh–ahhh–can try."

Emma pulled Elizabeth up the hill.

Halfway up the hill a sign reading, "Paxton Hotel" blared in her face. The hotel was simply a large white tent. Maybe there would be some help inside.

Almost tripping over the ropes that held the canvas, Emma lifted the flap.

"May I help you?" a man asked.

Elizabeth gasped and bent over, clutching her huge belly as a gush of water ran down her legs.

# 17

# *The Birth*

EMMA PULLED ELIZABETH BEHIND the tent flap. The children had tagged after them, and were now whining for their supper. Emma said, "You young'uns set yourself outside this tent and don't move until I say so!" They started at her unusual harsh manner and obeyed her.

Elizabeth was between contractions. She felt fine. "I'm fine, Emma, truly I am. Let's go to the Land Office." However, she knew the words were not true. Everyone knew that when the water broke, the baby would follow. She started shaking out of panic. Maybe the baby would just fall from between her legs and land right here on the dirty, muddy grass.

"Elizabeth, be quiet! Is there a doctor in this place?" Emma looked at the man behind a "desk" made of stacked wooden crates.

"I'm afraid I don't know, ma'am." He looked nervous.

"Well, you give me a room!" She threw some money at him.

"Very well, ma'am." He gestured for them to follow. He led them outside the tent to another canvas structure, even smaller. A worn quilt lay on the ground.

"Is this what you call a room?"

"Surely, ma'am you understand we are in the process of building our hotel." He pointed to some laborers hurriedly pounding nails into some rough boards.

"ARGHH" Elizabeth moaned.

"Get out!" Emma yelled at the man. She lowered Elizabeth to the dirty blanket. "Rest here. I got to tend the children."

Jenny and Johnny sat crying their eyes out, scared as little rabbits. Emma moved into their midst and they clung to her filthy skirts. "Now listen, Mrs. Duncan is not well, so I must care for her. You will stay right here. Now, Jenny, you mind Johnny. Don't go anywhere and don't talk to no one. Have you seen Doc?" Jenny shook her head.

She had no choice but to leave them on the other side of the tent flap. She ducked under the flap as Elizabeth moaned.

"Go ahead and yell, Lizzie. No one will hear you over the noise of this crazy place." Emma held Elizabeth's head in her strong hands. What would she do? She needed boiling water, instruments, rags, and she had nothing. She began ripping apart her one remaining petticoat. She stuck her head inside the main tent and ordered the man to get her some water. He was too scared not to obey her.

He returned with a bucket of red-tinted water. "This is water?"

"It's river water. All we have."

"You must have a knife on you somewhere."

The timid man pulled a filthy knife out of his vest pocket, "I need this back when you're uh done with it." He backed away as quickly as he could.

"Where is the Doc?" asked Elizabeth. Sweat poured from her head. "He was on the train. He has to be in townnnnnnnn." The last word was a scream as another contraction ripped through her. "Emma-Emma-I'm-going-to-die!"

"You ain't gonna die!"

"Emma, help me! Help me!" Elizabeth screamed again. "You–and–Jessie–didn't–tell–me–it–felt–like–this." She said between clenched teeth.

"I know, Lizzie, darling, but no one can describe the pain. You'll forget it once the young'un is here, I promise."

Hours passed. Emma spent her time checking on the children and trying to comfort Elizabeth. A well-meaning older woman had brought the children water and a loaf of bread. Darkness began to descend. The noise of the birth of the town and the noise of the birth of the baby blended. Finally, Elizabeth screeched,

"I think I feel it comin' out!"

"That means you got to push. Push it out, Lizzie."

"I can't. It hurts too bad." Elizabeth whimpered. "I can't! I'm splitting apart!"

Emma held Elizabeth's shoulders and told Elizabeth to grab both legs and push. Elizabeth felt she was ripping apart. Yet she had no choice but to push against the pain.

"Ah Ah Ah!" She pushed and pushed for what seemed like years.

Emma moved to look for the crowning of the head.

"I see the head, Lizzie, we're almost there! Push!"

With strength she did not know she had Elizabeth gave one last huge push. "Ahhhh!"

"Stop, stop, let me cut the cord."

Emma grabbed the knife and cut. Elizabeth heard a cry. Her baby's cry. The most beautiful sound she had ever heard.

"Oh, honey child, it's a girl, it's a baby girl." Emma wiped her carefully with the shredded petticoat, and then wrapped her in her own shawl, handing her to Elizabeth.

"Oh, Emma, she's perfect, she's just perfect." Elizabeth held her close while Emma did her best to clean the mess with very few supplies.

"Children you come in here and see this new baby." Under the flap came Jenny and Johnny. They smiled and laughed.

"Whatcha gonna call her?" asked Jenny.

"Hope. Cause that's what she represents. Hope for the future. She has given it to me."

"Here, honey, let me show you how to feed her." Emma undid Elizabeth's dress front and put Hope on the breast. Soon she was sucking away, oblivious to the fact that her mother owned nothing but the dress on her back and had nowhere to put her save her own arms. *Not even a manger like Baby Jesus,* thought Elizabeth. *Well, God, what are we going to do now? I can't get a claim, it's too late. How about a miracle now?*

*I've already given you one.* She almost heard God speak. *Yes, this baby is a miracle. She is alive and healthy after all this travel.* Her fledgling faith told her God could surely provide a place for them to live if he could bring a healthy human being into a city that was rising above her even as she prayed.

# 18

## *The Dilemma*

THE HOTEL OWNER HAD managed to find them a few blankets and pillows. They all bundled down for the night. Thankfully Johnny and Jenny slept through the baby's cries. Thankfully Jessie had had the forethought to make sure Elizabeth had packed some flannel diapers in her small carpetbag. The few flannel diapers and a couple of shirts she had sewn, along with a tiny quilt were all that the baby had. But it was better than nothing.

"Ladies, you got to pay me for another day or get out." The owner said through the flap.

"Well, can you give us a few moments to gather our things?"

"Hmph."

Elizabeth felt as if she had run a race across the land she had just crossed, or maybe the horses that had raced yesterday had raced over *her*. She tried to stand.

"No, you stay where you are." Emma pushed her gently back onto the worn blankets.

"But, Emma, we have to leave. We don't want to waste our little bit of money on this."

"How can he expect anyone to pay for a stay in a tent is beyond me."

"But he thinks he can, and he will throw us out."

Emma looked at the children huddled in a tangled heap, against Elizabeth's back, like kittens against their mama. Hope suckled, contended. Elizabeth looked down, wishing they were all so well taken care of. *But you are*, God whispered.

"Let's pray, Emma."

Emma looked at Elizabeth, shocked. She had never heard those words come out of Elizabeth's mouth.

"Well, that's what you're always saying."

"Yes, it is, but *you* have never said it."

"Well, it's time I do. You are always saying to trust God. I am trying, but are you?"

Emma, taken aback at Elizabeth's declaration of faith, sat down and started praying aloud. The children woke, but they were used to their stepmother's prayers and remained silent. Elizabeth silently joined her.

"God, you know we're in a fix. We got this far but we don't know what to do now. Sam's out there looking for land, Jessie's out there doing who knows what, and well, we need to know what to do next. Show us. We believe you can take care of us as you have always done, please God, in Jesus' name we ask it, we claim it, Amen.

"Amen!" said the children in unison. Elizabeth laughed.

"Well, now we wait for God's answer," Emma said. Then she left, muttering something about finding water. Elizabeth moved Hope to the other breast, wincing in pain as she felt a contraction. *I thought those were done yesterday.*

An hour later, Emma arrived with a bucket of red, muddy water holding a ball of dough.

"What in the world?"

"A woman washing down at the creek told me to do this. She said you put the dough in the water and let it set. Then the dough soaks the red dirt. Then you boil and strain the water, and drink it."

"Is there not a well in this town?"

"Some men are digging one on every corner, but nothing yet."

Elizabeth shuddered. This had to be the worse yet.

"And you'll never guess who I ran into out there."

"Who?"

"Doc Sims. He was in line for his claim. Says he got one close to town. He asked that we come on out there. He also hired some men to build a soddy."

"Where'd he get the money?"

Emma put her hands on her hips. "Now, Elizabeth, you know Doc has his ways."

Elizabeth remembered his excursion into Lexington. Gambling.

"That man!"

"Listen, Elizabeth, I'm not one to approve of card playing, but he seems to be our only answer to prayer at the moment. I'm not planning on questioning the Almighty's ways."

Elizabeth was too weary to argue. The old Elizabeth would have added living on money obtained by gambling on her list of sins sending her to hell, but the new Elizabeth decided to count her blessings.

"Now if only that man had been here yesterday when we needed him!" Emma exclaimed.

"Now, Emma, you did just fine delivering my baby."

"Thank God."

"Emma, I think Doc was in with some Sooners. That's how he got that plot."

"Like I said, Elizabeth, let's not be questioning the Almighty's, or Doc's ways."

"Any sign of Sam, Jessie, or. . .?"

"Jared?" Emma finished her sentence.

"None." Emma tried not to show her concern. "Maybe they went to Kingfisher to file. You never know what might happen out there."

"But we agreed to all meet here in Guthrie."

"Let's have faith, Lizzie. For now, let's gather the young'uns and go find Doc. At least he won't charge us two bits an hour for sitting in his tent."

Elizabeth tried to breathe but the pain kept stealing her breath. Emma managed to gather the children and shove them back inside the tent. Then she trudged off to find Doc. Later she told Elizabeth what happened. Emma had found Doc, still in line.

"Doc, I'm worried about Elizabeth. We got to get her off that ground or she'll surely take a fever after having that baby."

"Water for a nickel!" A filthy ten–year–old boy held out a dipper to Emma.

"A nickel!" She shooed the boy away. He moved on down the line. Emma was amazed to see people pull out money to pay for a drink of filthy water. She returned her attention to Doc.

"Well, Emma, I told her to find a man to take care of her once."

"Yeah, well, Doc, you happened to be that man right now! You got to do something."

"How's am I supposed to get this claim filed if I leave now? Then what we gonna do?" He spat a stream of tobacco. "You seen Sam?"

"No. You are the only hope we have. I told Elizabeth you'd let us camp on your claim."

"Do you think I'm some henpecked old biddy that will do whatever you womenfolk say?"

Emma crossed her arms and stared into his beady little dark eyes. The man behind Doc guffawed.

"That your woman?" He looked at Doc.

"No, thank the Lord, she ain't."

"Well, are you wanting a man?" He winked at Emma, and his toothless grin made her stomach ill.

Emma gave him a look that would have killed a toad and ignored him. "Doc, I know you got money. Give me some and I'll hire a team to get us out of this crowd. Sam will pay you back."

"With what? His good looks? Oh, what the heck, you know I'm joshing', here's two dollars. Go get Elizabeth a wagon and some food. When I get this filed, I'll find you."

"We're at that hotel." She pointed at the mess of tents. "The Paxton. Follow the signs." Doc shrugged. Emma threw up her hands; put the money in her apron pocket and marched off, looking for a wagon to hire.

As she pushed through the crowd, she heard a woman exclaim, "Emma!"

She looked up, and around but saw no one she recognized. Maybe she had imagined it. She was so tired. She pushed on.

"Emma, Emma!"

This time she stopped dead in her tracks. She knew that voice.

"Mildred!"

Mildred's kind, round face stood out from the crowd. She held open her arms. Emma ran. In the midst of this horrid, stinking town, she had found a friend.

Mildred held her at arm's length. "Where's everyone else?" They both spoke at once, then laughed. "You first," Mildred said.

"Oh Millie, you just don't know. Emma's tears fell. She had held them back for so long. Mildred's dark brown eyes under her bonnet filled with concern.

"What, oh what? Is it Lizzie?"

"Millie, she's had her baby. She's back there in a filthy tent and I just got to get her out of here."

Mildred was the type to take charge when taking charge was needed. She gripped Emma's arm firmly and said, "Where is she?"

"But Mil—what about your children, your man? Where are they?"

"They are standin' in line—over there. Just let me go tell them I need the wagon."

Emma took a deep breath, but she did not let Mildred out of her sight. She would never find her again. She followed as close as she could until she saw Mildred's family: their auburn heads and freckled faces had never looked so dear.

George, Becky, and Jacob all embraced her, and questions flew around her ears. She didn't answer any. She let Mildred explain to George while she took some deep breaths, inside trying to calculate how to stretch the two dollars to buy enough supplies to last as long as she could. Finally, Mildred pulled her back to the present.

"Come, Emma, I will take you to our wagon and help you get Lizzie on it."

"But I don't know where to take her!"

"We'll think of something!" They grabbed hands and pushed their way through the crowd.

\*\*\*

In the darkness outside the city, Sam bent down and tried to read the claim numbers on the stake in front of him, but it was too dark. He lit a match. Ouch! It burnt out before he could see anything. Why hadn't he brought along a candle? He lit another match. If only he knew his letters and numbers. He pulled the carefully hoarded piece of brown store paper from his inner jacket pocket and pulled the stub of pencil from another pocket. He would just have to copy the claim number and hope he matched the numbers correctly. Aenohe, who had ridden next to him the entire day without a word, picked up some cow chips and set them near the claim inscription. He lit a match, dropping it into the chips. Aenohe took the paper, copied the numbers, and handed it back to Sam.

"Thank ya, boy; sure glad I brought you along." But worry filled his heart. If only he had made it before dark. What if someone else had been here before? He could not see any tracks near the stone, but they could have blown away already. Should he attempt to make it to Guthrie tonight? He could not.

"Guess we better stay put till morning, Boy."

Aenohe undid his blanket and lie down, fast asleep in no time. Not able to behold a foot in front of him when the tiny fire died, Sam pulled his bedroll off of his horse and lay down with his Winchester in his arms. But he did not sleep.

\*\*\*

Somehow Mildred and Emma managed to lift Elizabeth and the baby into the wagon. The children crowded around her. Emma ordered Jenny to hold the baby while she held onto Elizabeth. Elizabeth tried to be grateful that she had friends around her, but her body ached, and her feet swelled, and she was beginning to feel hot.

"Emma, I thought feet only swelled during pregnancy, not after."

"Lizzie, my feet swell something fierce after each time I had my babies. You must stay put, stop trying to walk about."

"But, Emma, I. . ."

Elizabeth settled back on the quilts as Emma instructed. The swelling simply had to go down. She had no time to be an invalid. She took a deep breath and wiped her face.

Elizabeth barely heard Mildred say to Emma, "We will take her to our claim. It's close to town."

"But you haven't filed it yet!"

"It don't matter. We don't have another choice." Emma handed the baby to Jenny and climbed over the wheel to sit next to Elizabeth. Mildred said, "Giddap," to the horses. They moved slowly through the crowd. Emma felt Elizabeth's forehead. She was burning up. The feared "childbed fever" had set in, even without the bed.

Mildred moved efficiently through the crowd. "We're out here just south of town next to the creek! The Lord surely helped us get the best claim."

"I only wish there were a cabin on it," said Emma.

"Cabin? You know there ain't wood for such things here. We'll build a soddy. But for now, we got that tent." Mildred and George were way more prepared than most folks. They must have had more money available. The children had all dropped off to sleep, the wagon being the most familiar setting they knew. The baby was quiet for the moment. Elizabeth's eyes opened and closed.

Mildred pulled past the claim marker and stopped next to the creek. She climbed down as Emma set the baby in the wagon bed. Emma climbed down herself and then reached over the side for the tent. She worked hard trying to pound the stakes into the tough red dirt. It was nearing late afternoon judging by the sun in the sky. "You best get back to town for your family, I can finish here." Emma said.

"I hate to leave you, deary, but you are right." Mildred wiped her hands on her apron, and said, "We'd best get Lizzie and the children off the wagon." Emma took a deep breath, rubbed the small of her back where it ached from bending over, and set herself to the task of moving the ailing Elizabeth. She hardly weighed more than a mite now that the baby was out of her. They gently lifted her, quilt and all, and carried her, one on each end until they settled her on the dirt floor. Mildred helped move the children and then she headed back to town.

Emma stood still for a moment watching her until she disappeared over the horizon. It was getting late and Emma wondered how she was going to manage. She made sure the Winchester was close. But she didn't have time to wonder. Johnny woke, yelling as usual. She held his hand and bade him help her gather cow chips for a fire. She lit the fire and did her best to settle the children. The only thing she had to offer them to eat was the hardtack she had bought this morning until she could get enough water boiling for beans. Poor dears, they were so exhausted. Elizabeth opened her eyes again and asked for water. She handed her a tin mug of the tepid, cloudy liquid. But she drank.

"Do ya think ya could feed the baby?"

"Give her here." Elizabeth struggled to sit.

"Na, you don't have to sit, here I'll show ya how to feed her lying down."

The baby's mouth was open for a scream, so Emma got her hungry little mouth attached. Elizabeth was awake enough to help just a little. Emma lay down next to the baby. Her eyes closed and sleep claimed her despite of the aches and pains in her every joint.

\* \* \*

Daylight had broken when they heard hoofbeats. Emma sat up and grabbed the gun. The children still slept. "What is it, Emma?" Elizabeth asked.

"Someone is coming." She tried not to think of claim jumpers.

"Probably just Mildred and George." Emma grabbed the gun, just in case.

"Emma?"

Sam.

Emma jumped with a shriek. The children woke suddenly and scrambled up with shouts of "Pa! Pa! Pa!" Elizabeth wished she could do the same, but Hope was firmly attached and would scream should she move an inch.

"Emma, you better fix that man some breakfast," Elizabeth said through the canvas.

"I'd fix him a feast if I had the food."

"I brought food! Enough for everyone." Sam said.

"He's got three rabbits, Lizzie!" Emma shouted.

"Wasn't me that shot the rabbits, it was Aenohe." Sam smiled. Elizabeth did not relish the thought of rabbit, but anything beat the tasteless hardtack they had eaten yesterday.

"Where's Doc?" asked Sam.

"Oh he's back in Guthrie in a saloon, holding a bottle of whiskey and a deck of cards, for sure," Emma said.

Hope finished nursing. Elizabeth buttoned her dress and tried to crawl from the tent.

"Emma, I have to stand. I'm stiff as a board." She said when Emma gave her the look that meant "Stay put."

But she helped her down, took the baby, and set her on a blanket. She did feel better. Emma hoped the fever had passed. She knew too many women who had not survived the dreaded childbed fever.

"Sam, did you file a claim?"

"Of course."

"Did you see Jared or Jessie in the line when you filed?"

"No, I ain't seen Jared or Jessie since the race."

"Don't worry, Lizzie," said Emma, "They could have gone to Kingfisher to file."

But Elizabeth fretted, chewed her nails, and tried not to imagine Jared face down, dead on the prairie with vultures eating his flesh.

"Sam, look at this baby. Isn't she just perfect?"

"She sure is. Reminds me of Jenny when she was born."

"Aw, Pa, I was never that tiny."

"Jenny, dear, you were tinier."

"We thought she'd never make it, but look at this tall, strong girl we got now."

Jenny beamed.

Sam butchered the rabbits and cooked them over the fire.

Elizabeth devoured the meat. It had been days since they'd had anything so nourishing.

"Now you just eat up, Lizzie, you gotta get your strength back," Emma said as she smacked Johnny's hand away from the fire.

"What if Jared is. . ." Elizabeth would not allow herself to finish the sentence.

"Now, you just stop your fidgeting." Sam patted her back. "He'll show up, and if he doesn't, me, Aenohe, and Doc will go look for him."

A few hours later as Elizabeth napped, she heard Doc's voice.

"Sam! 'bout time you showed up. Did you get a claim?"

"You betcha, but it's a few miles from here."

"Doc, you seen Jared or Jessie?" Elizabeth sat to listen closely.

"Na, ain't seen hide nor hair of either, Sam." Concern clouded his voice.

"What you think we should do?" asked Sam.

"I'd say give it another day and then we go looking for them."

I got to get to my claim, or it'll be jumped for sure," said Sam. "Maybe Aenohe & I should go look today."

"Don't know where to start, Sam, this territory is as wide as the ocean." Emma remarked.

"Well, I'm going to ride to town and ask around." Sam must have walked away because the conversation ended. Elizabeth bit a nail. Would she be this worried about Jared if she did not love him? And what about Jessie? She had been the mother Elizabeth never had. She'd had way too many losses in her life, and she could not take one more, not one more. Tears filled her eyes.

Sam and Aenohe returned at sundown. No sign of Jared. Elizabeth's heart fell to her shoes. Tears dropped on Hope's fuzzy head before she could wipe them away. She wondered what was keeping Mildred and George. After all, it was their claim. Doc rode in late in the afternoon.

Doc sat on his haunches heating coffee over the fire. Emma was putting the children to bed in the tent.

"You hear anything?" Doc voiced what Elizabeth was afraid to say.

"Nothing. I went in every saloon in town and asked everyone who would listen. A couple men offered to go looking—for a price, of course."

"Come morning, I'm going out there. I told Jessie not to do this. She won't listen to no one." Doc said.

"I'm going with you."

"Sam, are we going to lose our claim?" asked Emma.

"I don't know, Emma."

"Well, I can go out there and hold it down."

"No, it's too dangerous. I can't let you go alone."

"Well, then let me go look for Jessie and Jared while you go to the claim." Emma sounded desperate.

"What about the young'uns? And Elizabeth?"

"You are right." Emma sat down with her hands on her head.

All of them crawled into their bedrolls, Doc, Aenohe, and Sam near the fire, guns nearby, and the women and children crowded into the tent. *Please, God, please, I beg you, please send my Jared back to me. Please let Jessie be alive. Please let us wake up to both of them riding into camp.* The crickets and cicadas' song, coupled with sheer exhaustion sent Elizabeth into a slumber, finally; with Hope nestled in her weary arms.

# 19

# *The Injury*

AT FIRST LIGHT THE camp stirred. Elizabeth scooted to peer from beneath the canvas to see no sign of Jared or Jessie. Doc, Aenohe, and Sam and the horses were gone. They must have left before dawn. Emma woke and dragged herself to start breakfast. The children woke and began their morning routine of the usual laughing and playing. Hope nursed; Elizabeth cried. How much more of this waiting could she take?

Thankfully the men had hauled a few buckets of water from the creek and today, they had enough to wash a few diapers, made from cheap flannel that Doc had brought from town. Emma filled a bucket and started scrubbing. She was not one to sit idle and worry. *Not like me,* thought Elizabeth.

"What if they never. . ."

"Now you just stop that, Lizzie. We will have faith. Let's pray again." Emma prayed aloud, ending with "God, please bring Jared and Jessie back to us."

When she said "Amen," Elizabeth stopped crying. She would try as hard as she could to have faith today. Just today. Surely by nightfall someone would bring word.

"Hullo there!" a distant voice caused Emma to jump and spill the water.

Then two horses came thundering into camp with the most welcome sights Elizabeth had ever seen. Jessie.

"Oh Jessie!"

Jessie jumped from the horse and then Elizabeth saw what Jessie had been carrying on the second horse.

Jared. "Oh my God! Jessie, is he dead? Emma rushed to the horse. Elizabeth's heart fell to her feet.

"He wasn't when I threw him up there a few hours ago."

"What happened?"

"Just help me get him down."

Emma and Jessie managed to get an unconscious Jared off the horse. Elizabeth saw blood caking his shirt and face.

"He's been shot. Just in the arm, and the bullet went clear through. I think he's out from loss of blood. Where's Doc?"

"He and Sam went looking for you two!" said Elizabeth

"Well, guess it's up to us womenfolk as usual."

Elizabeth handed the baby to Jenny. She took a knife and cut Jared's shirt, peeling it carefully from his body. She flushed as she cut through the shredded cotton to reveal his muscular chest.

Emma went to the bucket and then heated water over the fire to bathe the wound. Jessie tied the horses. Emma held Jared's head, took a wet rag and ran it over Jared's mouth. She dripped some drops into his charred and chapped lips.

"Jessie, where'd you find him?" asked Elizabeth.

"Right outside Guthrie after I filed my claim. He was on the ground near Cottonwood Creek. Probably someone shot him to get his claim."

"Then he didn't get one," Elizabeth said.

"Not unless he filed it before he got shot, which I doubt."

"I got one, Lizzie, and darn good one too. Close to town and the creek. I'm going back out there to hold it."

"Now?"

"Well, in a few hours," said Jessie, "You girls seen that town?"

"Not since the day of the run."

"It's a real town now. Not just tents. There are buildings everywhere, most of them saloons." Jessie stopped short, looked at Elizabeth, then at Jenny holding the baby. "You—you?"

"Yes, Jessie," said Emma, crossing her arms, "Lizzie had that baby in a filthy tent on April 22. She went into labor as we were pulling into Guthrie station. And yes, I delivered her with no help from Doc or anyone else. Where in the world did you go after we got on that train?"

Jessie's wry look provoked laughter in Elizabeth. As least she could laugh now. Jessie's stream of tobacco left her mouth as she sputtered, "Well, at least I got me a claim! And better you than me, Emma, I ain't never delivered no baby."

"Well, I hadn't either! I'd only remembered what the midwife did when I had my babies."

Jessie took the baby from Jenny. "What's her name?"

"Hope."

"Now, that's a good name. She's beautiful, Lizzie, you did real good."

"Thanks, Jessie."

Jared moaned.

"He's coming to, Jessie, get some water." Emma rushed to his side. Jessie brought a tin cup and Emma held Jared's head and let him drink. Jared's eyes opened. Elizabeth held his hand.

"Where? What?"

"You been shot, Jared," said Emma. "You just rest after you drink some." He closed his eyes.

"Yeah, he'll live," said Jessie. "That boy has a constitution of iron."

Elizabeth cried again. This time they were tears of joy. Now if only Sam, Aenohe, and Doc would return they would all be together again.

"Jessie, when you going to tell us how you got that claim?" asked Jenny, Johnny on her hip.

"Boy, do I got a tale to tell, sweetie, but first let's care for the horse and get Jared settled," Jessie moved the wad to her left cheek and stomped off. Elizabeth noted Jessie's trousers were covered in red dirt, and that she limped when she walked.

"Elizabeth."

"Yes, Jared. But please don't try to talk. You're hurt."

"I didn't get a claim."

"Ssh. It doesn't matter."

"Yes, it does." He coughed. He flinched as his injured shoulder moved.

"See, now, Jared, I told you not to talk." He let his head fall back and closed his eyes. Elizabeth smoothed his tangled curls, and then her hand ran along his solid jaw, feeling the rough stubble even through her thick calluses. *She loved him. No. She could not. But she did. Oh, what was she going to do?* Then Hope cried, her milk let down, and duties claimed her thoughts.

A few hours later Jared opened his eyes again. This time Elizabeth managed to get some broth made from boiling the rabbits' bones into his mouth. He did not speak, but his eyes said what his mouth did not. *Thank you.*

Instead of crawling into the tent next to Jessie, she lay Hope next to her and fell asleep with her head on Jared's good arm. This was how Emma found her in the morning.

"Girl, wake up, your baby's starved!"

Elizabeth moved to take the screeching infant as Emma sat next to Jared.

Jared was awake. Emma spooned some broth into his mouth.

"I didn't get a claim."

"You said that already."

"I didn't get a claim."

"Jared, you didn't get a claim. Neither did half of the others that started off half-cocked last week."

"But now I can't. . ."

"You can't what?"

Elizabeth's ears perked.

"Nothing."

"You can't what?" Elizabeth asked.

"I can't stay in this territory. That's what!"

"Now, now don't go getting all riled up, Jared!" Emma tried to calm him.

"All my plans. They are dead. They are gone." He struggled to rise.

"No, Jared, please stay put." Elizabeth cried, *please Jared, don't hurt yourself worse, please. I love you.* She thought them but did not speak them. Doc appeared from across the ridge.

"What in tarnation?" declared Doc as he beheld Jared lying next to the fire.

"He's been shot, and he's upset. Will you do something to calm him?" begged Elizabeth. "He's going to tear his wound."

Doc pulled out his ever-present flask of whiskey. "This is all I got."

"Just do something!"

Doc offered the flask to Jared and said, "Here, Boy, this'll calm you." Jared shook his head.

"You know I don't drink, Doc."

"Even the good Lord drank wine, Jared, and the Apostle Paul told Timothy to take it for his stomach. It's all the medicine I got." But Jared refused what was offered. Instead he simply went silent and closed his eyes.

Elizabeth left him in Emma and Doc's capable hands and climbed into the tent with Hope. She snuggled into the quilts and sobbed as Hope slept. Jared was hurt and she could do nothing to fix it. Jared had gotten no land and his dreams were dead. She had not convinced anyone to file a town lot for her. What would they do and where would they go now? She cried into the worn blanket under her. Strength and determination had been based on the hope of a future here in Oklahoma Territory. Now there was no future, only once again she was dependent upon her friends. And the strongest friend of all was injured.

*God, you gotta do something. I am really trying to have the faith that Emma taught me, but I am at the end of my rope and I can't hang on much longer. Thank you for my darling baby. What am I going to do? How am I going to support her?*

# 20

# *Jessie's Tale*

"Jessie, you are joshing! There is no way that tale could possibly be true!" Elizabeth heard Emma and Jessie bantering when she awoke the next morning.

"What now, you two?" She said as she stood to her feet, Hope wrapped in a blanket snuggled in her arms. Her glance took in Jared next to the fire. He was asleep.

"How do you think I got this bum ankle?" She took off her boot and showed Emma and Elizabeth the swollen limb, covered in varying shades of periwinkle and violet.

"Stumbling from the train?" asked Elizabeth. "We lost sight of you as soon as we found the only seat left in that crazy circus of a Boomer train."

Emma stirred the beans over the fire and shook her head in disbelief. "I believe you got a claim, Jessie, because I've seen the paper, but I do not believe the manner in which you say you obtained it."

Elizabeth shifted Hope to other hip and sat down, accepting a tin cup of beans from Emma. Jessie crossed her legs, still clad in the ugly canvas trousers and took a fresh chaw of tobacco from her ever-present tin.

"I jumped off the train, Emma, that's all there is to it."

"But you would have been killed!"

"Landed in some soft sand."

"Jessie, really, just tell us the truth," pleaded Elizabeth.

"I am tellin' you the truth, so help me God with my hand on the Bible! I jumped off the front of that train just south of Guthrie with my claim stake in my hand. I drove the stake in, tied my old petticoat to the stake, and then fired my gun into the air! Everyone on that train heard me say, 'I claim this land for Jessie Shows!' Then Jeremiah stuck out his arm and helped me hop the caboose."

Emma still shook her head in disbelief. "I will have to hear an eyewitness before I believe you, Jessie."

"Jeremiah was on the train? We haven't seen him since Purcell." Elizabeth asked.

"Tarnation, 'course he was. He's got him a townsite. Guess he's going to open a feed store. And there were hundreds of other witnesses. Doc heard me for sure."

"Then why did he not say anything when I found him in line?" Emma inquired.

"How should I know why that snake does what he does?"

Jessie surprisingly did not try to convince Emma further. She was too stressed about getting back to her claim before someone stole it. After breakfast she said good–bye. She had still had no word on her son, Amos, but had managed to find some men to hire to build a soddy on her claim. Thankfully Jessie's land was only a mile south of town.

"Where did you get the money to pay anyone, Jessie?" asked Elizabeth

"Remember, I sold one horse and my wagon? Well, I had two rings left by my mother. I sold them too." Elizabeth shook her head full of tangled brown curls. Jessie would never cease to amaze her. All this time she had kept those rings a secret.

"The soddy is built. You are coming with me." Jessie told Elizabeth.

"I can't leave Jared."

"He's coming too."

"We can't move him yet."

PART FOUR: OKLAHOMA TERRITORY

Jessie's stream of tobacco hit the fire, "He'll be fine in a few days. I got to go." She mounted her horse and headed towards town. Her hat flew back, and her wild salt and pepper hair blew in the wind. Elizabeth noted what a lovely picture her silhouette made against the multi-colored sunset. The land may be harsh, but it was beautiful.

## 21

# *The Last Miles*

Two days later, Emma, Aenohe, and the children began the walk towards town as Sam had asked. Jessie had returned with a borrowed wagon, but it had no room for all of them. "A walk will do us good," Emma said. Jessie shrugged. Sam would meet them in Guthrie and fetch them to his own claim. There were promises of meeting Sunday at the Methodist Church tent. Oh, how she would miss Emma. George and Mildred and the children had finally come. George had brought a plow and with everyone's help, they had managed to build a one–room soddy. They put the tent canvas over it for now, until they could build a roof. It offered more shelter than they had had in so long.

"It ain't much, but it's a mite better than this old leaky sieve," she gestured to the canvas tent they had slept in for a week. Jared, sitting for the first time since his accident, tried a smile. Jared's optimism had returned slowly, along with his physical strength.

George and Mildred helped Jared onto the wagon bed. Elizabeth clambered to the seat and Mildred handed her Hope, wrapped in her only worn blanket. Elizabeth felt the dampness under Hope's back. She had wet her only dry diaper. There was nothing she could do about it, so she simply said nothing. The child would be raw with rash. She wanted to kick her feet on the ground and scream. Raising a baby in a soddy? It had to be better than a wagon or a tent.

Jared moaned involuntarily as the wagon bumped over the short, rough grass just starting to cover the red dirt. Spring flowers bloomed here and there.

When had she realized she loved this man? She did not know. She only longed to spend the rest of her life in his arms. *God, he has to survive. You can't take him because I need him. I can't live without him. You can't have him. You can't have him.* She ordered God. Emma had told her to *ask*, but she was beyond asking. She *ordered*.

* * *

"There it is," Jessie pointed to a mound on the prairie. Elizabeth made no sound. Nothing mattered anymore. She could barely keep her seat; she was so worn and weary. She turned to check on Jared. His eyes were closed, hopefully in sleep and not unconsciousness.

# 22

# *The Soddy*

A WEEK LATER, JARED was up, doing his share of the chores, even if it was slowly. Jessie had been to town and came thundering back, her horse heaving, waving something in the wind.

"It's half yours." Jessie waved an official-looking paper under Jared's nose. Jared grabbed it, tried to read it, stumbled at the words, and handed it back to her. "What does it say?"

"It says that you are half owner of the Double J Ranch."

"Double J?"

"Jessie and Jared. Sorry, Elizabeth could not think of a way to put the 'E' in it.

Elizabeth was still speechless. Jessie had deeded half of her claim to Jared?

"Jessie, I can't take it. . ."

"Sure you can. How am I supposed to run this spread on my own? You have cattle down in Purcell; I have the land to support them. It's a partnership, fifty–fifty. Now, you two make your wedding plans. We'll build another soddy so you can have your privacy."

Jared just stared, turned red. Elizabeth slipped under the worn quilt that doubled as a door with Hope in her arms and stared at the distant clouds. *Marriage? Of course, she loved him, but they had even spoken of courtship.* Her face burned.

She heard Jessie and Jared continue to argue. She knew in the end that Jessie would win. Jared had his pride, but Jessie had determination and stubbornness. She still didn't know about marriage. Love was one thing, but trust? Could she trust hers and Hope's future to Jared?

"Marriage, Jessie?" Jared yelled. "We haven't even courted. How could you say that in front of her?"

"Courtship Smourtship, Jared, how can you court someone when you live in the same soddy with her? I'll go and get one of those circuit–riding preachers hanging around town and bring him out here to marry you tomorrow!"

"Elizabeth deserves the respect of a courtship and a wedding."

"She don't care, Jared, I tell you."

At that point, Elizabeth decided to walk away. She continued her trek away from the soddy. She could not bear to hear more. Yes, she should interfere with this discussion; after all, it was about her future. But she simply didn't have the strength.

\* \* \*

It was Jessie's step, not Jared's that she heard behind her.

"Lizzie?"

"What?"

"You shouldn't be out, there'll be a chill settling soon and. . ."

"Jessie, how could you assume that Jared and I would marry? You were way out of line!"

"It's about time somebody said something! The way you two look at each other. . ."

"It's too soon, and I-I-I just can't. . ."

"Look, Lizzie, I'm just trying to help. Out here there just ain't time or energy for normal proprieties. Courting? Why that's just impossible."

"That's not what I mean. I don't care about courting. I am just not ready to marry."

"Well, what else are you going to do?"

"Get a job."

"With a baby? Not even that new school board is going to hire a widow with a baby to teach."

"I can take in laundry or sew."

"When you have a healthy, good-lookin' man ready to marry you?"

"Jessie, surely you of all people know I need to take care of myself."

"Law, girl, I give up." Jessie stomped back to the soddy.

A half an hour later, Elizabeth made herself enter the soddy. There was nowhere else to go. Jared lay asleep. She was glad she would not have to face him. She sat on the floor and nursed Hope as Jessie handed her a tin cup of beans. As soon as she ate, she curled up in the quilts next to Hope and slept.

In the morning, when she awoke, she leaned over to pick up Hope from the quilt next to her but instead, she screamed. Instead of Hope, some sort of animal stared at her. It took off running and burrowed into a hole in the wall before she could get out the door. Jessie came running, holding Hope.

"Land sakes, girl, whatcha hollerin' for?"

"It-it was an animal. I thought it got Hope!" she stuttered, pulling the baby from Jessie's arms. Jessie laughed.

"It was probably just a gopher or a prairie dog. We are living in their space."

"Jessie, I can't stand it. I just can't live with animals."

"Well, I'll put some fabric up for a sort of ceiling. I hear that keeps the critters from dropping on the floor."

"It came through the wall!"

Jessie sauntered to the hole and shoved some dirt and rocks into it. Hope cried and Elizabeth rocked her back and forth.

"Where's Jared?" Elizabeth asked when Hope's cries had succumbed to hiccups.

"He left."

"Where did he go?" Panic arose in her throat as she peered through the make- shift clothes-line full of diapers to the distant horizon.

"Let him take one of my horses to fetch his cattle and wagon from Purcell and our supplies. Probably take a week or two."

"He is not well enough!" *Maybe it was for the best*, Elizabeth thought. He wasn't ready to discuss marriage any more than she was. They needed time. But oh, how she missed him.

"We are not going to sit around mooning for what we do not have." Jessie declared.

"What are we going to do besides wash diapers?"

"We are going to go to town and buy some flannel, so we don't have to wash diapers every other hour–and some muslin for the ceiling. Then we got a meeting to attend."

"A church meeting?" Jessie did not attend church.

Jessie spit. "You know me better than that."

"Well, then what?"

"It's a temperance meeting. Womenfolk plan to make liquor illegal in this town."

"Let's go."

Elizabeth was all for anything that kept men from drinking.

# 23

# *Amos*

Two weeks had passed and still, Jared had not returned, nor had they heard anything. There were telegraph offices in Purcell, and now Guthrie had one, but Elizabeth knew Jared did not have the few cents it took to send one. She kept busy tending to Hope and helping Jessie plant a garden. Jessie did the hard work of breaking the sod with a sharp hoe and Elizabeth planted seeds.

They had attended the organization of the Guthrie branch of the Women's Christian Temperance Union at the Methodist Church. There were rumors of Carry A. Nation, the famous temperance champion from Kansas visiting Guthrie. Elizabeth hoped she would. She had heard that Carry could drive liquor out of a town. Tonight, there was another meeting and she intended to be there.

As they walked into the church, the telegraph operator handed Jessie a telegram.

*Jared.* Her heart jumped to her throat.

Jessie opened it. Then she dropped it. Her face white.

"Is it Jared?"

"Amos is dead."

Jessie sat limply down; Elizabeth next to her. Hope fussed, but Elizabeth had nowhere to set her. She patted Jessie's back with her free hand.

"What–?"

Jessie's shaking hand shoved the crumbled paper in Elizabeth's open one. "Amos Shows deceased. Stop. Evidence he was shot by federal agents. Stop. Trying to gain access to a claim before the run. Stop. Signed Purcell Sheriff. Stop"

So, Amos had been a Sooner, and died for it.

"We should go home, Jessie. You're way too upset to stay."

"No." Jessie pulled Elizabeth down to the seat as she tried to stand. "Stay put! Amos would have never done such a thing if he didn't drink himself. We are staying."

Pulling her feet beneath her, Elizabeth strained to listen. The church was wall–to–wall women, buzzing with excitement.

"We have word Carry A. Nation will be here within a week! And Moses Weinburg has agreed to let her speak in his saloon!" The cheering almost lifted the newly shingled roof.

# 24

# *The Saloon*

A WEEK LATER THEY gathered in the Same Old Moses Good Times Saloon at 115 West Harrison Street. There was still no word from Jared and now it had been three weeks. After leaving Hope with Emma in a cafe across the street, Elizabeth allowed excitement to rise in her breast. She had so looked forward to hearing Carry A. Nation speak. Carry could show them! She could show them how they could drive out liquor from this town. As she and Jessie entered the saloon, horrific smells of liquor met her nose. Of course, that was to be expected, but she still gagged. However, she wanted to chuckle when she saw Moses Weinburg, the owner looking squeamish. Perhaps fear dominated his thoughts. She had heard he allowed them to hold the meeting here in hopes of gaining publicity. More and more women crammed into the small frame building until the room looked about to burst at the seams. The few men who had been here when they arrived began tugging at their collars, looking nervous. Perhaps they had heard of Carry's reputation. She was not known for her serenity. But Elizabeth knew that Carry had promised to be civil to Moses.

Elizabeth had never been inside a saloon. She noted the gritty sawdust under her feet. The few men gathered round rough tables with cards in their hands, whisky bottles next to them. Jessie nudged and pointed a thumb at Doc and Jeremiah in a corner with a handful of cards and a cigar, then purposely ignored them when they waved and grinned. Elizabeth smiled and waved anyway. Elizabeth wanted to speak to them, but could not get through the crowd. Spots of tobacco littered the sawdust. She narrowly avoided stepping in a wad. She shuddered.

Carry stomped to the front of the room. A tall woman, she stood at least six feet, stout and strong, dressed in a severe black dress and bonnet. When she began to speak no one noticed Carry's appearance. Carry's voice immediately to gained control of the room. Elizabeth stood mesmerized. This woman had so much charisma, so much power. She began her speech with, "God has sent me to rid the Territory of the evils of drink! Oklahoma Territory must be saved! There are twenty–four saloons here in Guthrie that we must annihilate."

*Twenty-four saloons built in one month?* She wondered how many churches had been built.

The room remained calm. Moses, behind the bar, looked relieved when she wound down her speech. Suddenly Carry pulled her famous hatchet from the belt that wrapped around her ample waist. Moses grunted in protest, rushing toward her. Carry threw the hatchet, and it landed on his brand–new hand–carved mahogany bar. He voiced his outrage.

"Carry! Why I ought to. . ." But it was too late. The women had taken Carry's action as a symbol for them to start their action.

Glasses began flying through the air. "CRASH! BANG! BOOM!"

Moses ducked behind the counter.

A few men managed to squeeze out the back door.

The women sang at the top of their lungs. "ONWARD CHRISTIAN SOLDIERS MARCHING AS TO WAR."

Elizabeth wondered what to do. Should she participate? All in a split second, she thought that perhaps this behavior was no better than the action exhibited by drunks. She turned to leave, but a familiar face caught her eye.

Shock moved into her being beginning at her eyes and ending at her toes. A shudder flew up her spine while intense nausea gnawed at her stomach. There, in the farthest corner, cigar in his right hand, cards in his left, sat Jared Davidson.

His eyes met hers. She turned, her skirts stirring up sawdust. She pushed her way through skirts and overturned tables, struggling to get to the swinging doors and out into the fresh air.

"Elizabeth! Wait!" She heard Jared's voice.

A sob choked at the back of her throat. The doors! Finally, pushing them open, she ran into the dusty street. A horse and buggy stood in front of the saloon. She avoided them.

"Elizabeth!" Jared's voice from the front of the saloon called out to her. She ignored it. The sobs shook her. Tears mixed with dust blinded her. She stumbled. That was all the time Jared needed to catch her. His strong hands grasped her elbows. She shoved him away.

"No, don't touch me!"

"Elizabeth, stop, please, listen to me. . ." His voice, out of breath just made her shake even harder.

"No, Jared, no, don't hit me!" She broke away from him, running.

"Elizabeth!" He caught her again. He pulled her into his muscular arms. She resisted, beating her fists on his chest.

"NO! NO! Don't!"

"Elizabeth!" He wouldn't let her go; his voice murmured comforting words until finally her struggling melted into hiccupping. Jared pulled her to the side of the road, pushing his way through the crowds of the fledgling town until they came to the end of the tents and freshly built lumber buildings to open prairie. He strode down the gentle rise in the prairie that was town, guided her along until they sat on the banks of Cottonwood Creek. The only trees for miles around gave a soothing effect to Elizabeth. The soft whisper of the wind rustling through the branches began to quiet her aching soul.

The water swirled in its red muddy state. She thought that her life events swirled like the water. Churning, rushing along daring anyone to catch them. Daring Jared. He tried, oh how he tried. His deep but compassionate voice broke through her shell.

"Elizabeth, Elizabeth, what's wrong? Please tell me. I'm sorry I didn't come straight to Jessie's to see you when I got back. Please forgive me. I'm sorry I didn't tell you I was leaving. I was just so confused." He pulled her into his arms once again. His gentle hands on her back tranquilized her racing heart. Finally, she could speak though the hiccups.

"I—uh-(gulp)-saw–you–drinking."

"Sarsaparilla."

"What?"

"I wasn't drinking whisky, beer, moonshine, or whatever else you're thinking I was doing."

"But—you—had a cigar. And you had cards."

"In case you haven't noticed, that's how the gentlemen of Guthrie do their business. I was trying to cut a deal about transporting my cattle to market." Jared explained. "I met him on the ride back from Purcell, and he was leaving town quickly, so I had to. . ."

A breeze blew the rest of her hairpins apart and her tangled brown tresses fell to her shoulders, and down to her waist. She felt her milk let down.

"Oh, no! Oh my!" She jumped up, tripping on her skirt.

"Elizabeth, calm down!"

"It's time to feed the baby. Emma has her."

"Well, we can't delay that." They stood. "Elizabeth?" He asked as they trudged back towards the tent city.

"Yes?"

"Does any of this have to do with why you won't talk about your past?"

Silence.

"Please, I want to help you."

She took a deep breath, "Yes, Jared, it does have something do with it."

"Well, that's a start, Elizabeth."

"Yes, the baby's father used to drink."

"Drink? How much? A shot of whiskey here and there?"

"No, Jared, he drank like–like–one of those drunks we run in that saloon. More than Doc or Jeremiah."

"So, you were married to a drunk. That's why you can't take it if you think someone is drinking around you." She sniffed, inhaling the fresh Oklahoma wind. "No."

"No? No, what?"

"Jared, I wasn't married to him."

Just then the noises of town surrounded their conversation. Shouts and hammers made it impossible to carry it any further. But his look said it all. *Shock? Hurt?* She allowed her eyelids to lift, her feet stopping as did his. Her blue eyes gazed into his, green like the grass near the creek. *What did she expect to see in those eyes? Hatred? Pity?*

Instead she found compassion. *Or was it love?*

His fist punched his other hand. He fingered the gun on his hip.

"I can't say more. I just can't."

"There, there." He just held her, silently. She was so glad he was home. She was so glad he was not drinking. But she must go feed the baby.

He walked her back to the Same Old Moses Saloon. Things had quieted down. Elizabeth saw no sign of Carry A. Nation. Instead she saw someone pounding a sign into the ground outside the saloon. She pulled Jared towards the sign so they could read it, "All nations welcome except Carry." They looked at each other and burst out laughing just as Jessie walked out the door of the saloon. Doc followed, slightly swaying, and laughing.

"Are you coming out to the claim?" Jessie asked Jared after showing her surprise to find him standing next to Elizabeth on the board sidewalk. Jessie shoved Doc away as he tried to put his arm around her.

"No, I got business here in town."

He patted Elizabeth on the shoulder and walked away.

*Tomorrow. Tomorrow she would tell him the truth.*

# 25

# *The Journal*

LATER THAN NIGHT, ELIZABETH sat, holding the baby. Hope slept peacefully. Elizabeth knew she should lay her down and go back to sleep herself, but the night was unusually warm and peaceful. Thoughts of Jared flitted across her mind. She had dreamed about him right before Hope woke up. She could not put words to the dream, only that she had felt Jared's presence. He had been by her side the whole trip. When he had not come in from the Land Run she had panicked. She was so used to him being around she had forgotten what it was like to live without him. *Was that it? Was he just a habit?* William had become a habit, but mostly a bad one. She was surprised that she could think of him without the pain shooting through her heart.

Elizabeth had hoped and prayed that Hope would not look like William, and so far her prayer had been answered. Elizabeth set the baby in her basket. She remembered how Jared had held her, and how small she had looked in his huge hands. The look he had given Elizabeth, lying pale and wan on the blanket had caused her weak heart to pound. Those piercing green eyes of his had always had that effect on her, but she had tried to ignore it. Now she could not. When he had not come, she thought her heart would stop. *Does that mean that I love him?* How could someone like her know what love is? She had thought she loved William. But now she could see it was just a puny, sickly, kind of admiration she had held for him. Nothing she had ever felt for anyone compared to her feelings for Jared. But then, Emma said that she could not base all of her decisions on feeling. She must think, but more importantly pray and search the Scriptures for answers. Dare she light the lamp and read? Would it wake Hope? She knew it wouldn't wake Jessie. Not even a twister would wake Jessie once she settled for the night. She decided she would risk it.

She could hear the katydids down by the creek, and a few bullfrogs croaking their love songs. But as she felt before, this night was exceptionally quiet. Pushing her long, loose, dark brown curls behind her ears, she stood up, the worn, but warm wedding ring patterned quilt that Emma had given her fell to the packed red dirt floor.

Elizabeth reached for the wooden crate she used for a table and fumbled in the dark for a match. Her hand closed around a matchbook and she struck it and lit the lamp. Next to the lamp, she found the black leather–bound Bible that Emma had loaned her. As she rustled through the thin pages, she passed the book of Psalms, then Proverbs, and then Ecclesiastes. She opened the Song of Songs. As she looked at the words, she remembered her pastor thundering from the pulpit that this book was not for children to read. Of course, that only made all the children go home and turn to it. She had read it as a child, but now, now she wished to see it as an adult.

She read verse 8:7 "Many waters cannot quench love, neither can the floods drown it: if a man would give all the substance of his house for love, it would utterly be contemned."

*Many waters cannot quench love.* This phrase was prettier than those fancy poems that Aunt Jane read. It was more beautiful than anything Jane Austen had ever written. Chewing a fingernail, she recalled Jared crossing the rivers on their trip. She remembered that morning that they had cried on the banks of the Canadian. The waters did not quench her love then.

Did Jared love her? Oh, she knew he cared. She knew he was a trusted friend. He would do anything she asked of him. But did he long for her as she longed for him? Did he long to share his life with her? He was the only man she had ever known that encouraged her to think and do for herself. He had been so proud when she had gotten the job in Purcell. But—but she had thought of William in much the same manner. She had thought that William was a thinker. He had laughed at the Women's Suffrage Movement but had never really spoken against it. Jared approved of it!

*What am I doing comparing them? They don't even compare!* She thought of how Jared reminded her of her father. Papa had been steady and sure, and had been on his own from a young age.

Emma had encouraged her to start writing a journal. "It's good for getting your thoughts out in the open." She had said before she and Sam had packed up the children and driven to their homestead, and now the journal lay on the crate. She had no desk as she had in Virginia, so she sat against the sod wall on the dirt floor. Hope still slept soundly, so Elizabeth decided to write. She took her one and only quill, dipped the quill into the dark liquid, and began to scratch her thoughts against the thin paper.

May 31, 1889

Guthrie, O.T.

*I think I'm in love with Jared Davidson. How childish that sounds! Not like a newly turned nineteen-year-old should sound. I am a woman now, with a child, and here I am with a schoolgirl crush. But I know. I know. It's really not a schoolgirl crush. I've always thought he is handsome, but never thought of him as more than a friend. Well, I think I did, but I was too hurt to admit it. The love has grown stronger and stronger as we journeyed across many counties, cities, and rivers to get here to Oklahoma Territory. I don't know if he loves me. He seems to care, but I don't know if that is love. Besides, I have a child. What man would want to raise a child that is not his?*

She paused and gazed once again at the sleeping Hope. She slept with her tiny fists pulled up next to her adorable cheeks.

Elizabeth leaned over the basket to caress her downy-soft head. She picked up the quilt off the floor and wrapped it around her legs. She nestled herself in the worn cotton folds and after re–dipping the quill in the ink continued to write.

> *I just read in the Bible tonight that many waters cannot quench love. Is God speaking to me about Jared? How do I know if God wants me to marry him? Would God just tell me? Emma said that once you become a Christian that God speaks to you, but he hasn't spoken to me. She says he uses other people and Scripture and prayer and sometimes preachers to speak to you and you have to stay close to him to know. I've been trying to read my Bible and pray every day. I went to the organization of the Methodist church last Sunday. I hope God is pleased with me, but I cannot be sure. The preachers I hear say an awful lot about God being angry with people. Emma says God loves me. I sure hope so. I hope he has forgiven me of having a baby without being married.*
>
> *Back to Jared. It has taken me a long time to realize that I love him. From the first time he scooped me up in his arms when I fainted, to the time he held me in the rain after Sally died, I felt drawn to him. He makes me feel so safe. But I knew that I just could not let myself get close to a man after William. But Jared was there. Always there. I long to live my life at his side, but I also long to prove to myself that I can make it on my own. I don't want to be like Jessie who swears she will never let a man court her again, but I do want to see women get to do things like vote and own land in every state. How can I want two things that are so different?*

She could tell it was getting near morning. Tired, she put both Bible and journal away, blew out the lamp, and tried to get at least an hour's more sleep before the morning work began.

As she perched next to the fire that morning, heating water to wash diapers and trying to stay awake, she continued to think of Jared. Hope lay awake in her basket at Elizabeth's feet but did not fuss. She heard hoofbeats in the distance. Elizabeth's pulse raced her breath left her.

"Good morning, Elizabeth." Jared held his hat in his hands. She noticed a few days growth on his face and wondered if he would let it grow. She hoped so. He had such a nice, full beard. He leaned over to talk to Hope. "Good morning, darling."

"Hello, Jared." She looked up. He reached down, pulled her to her feet and to himself.

"Where's Jessie?"

"Off in the distance gathering cow chips."

"Got Doc and a few men to come out and put up some fence."

"When?"

"Tomorrow. Today I spend with you."

So much remained unspoken between them. It did not seem to matter as his green eyes bore holes into her blue ones.

Did he know that she had finally admitted to herself that she loved him?

"I was wondering if you would join me on a buggy ride this evening." Was he asking her to go 'a' courting'?"

"Where did you get a buggy?" He did not answer, just walked towards Jessie who had just come into sight.

Two thoughts ran through her mind: he would make an excellent father, and oh how she wished he would kiss her! She blushed.

His thick trousers could not hide muscular legs and his jacket of brown leather strained at his biceps. She watched him walk away and knew. She knew. She loved him. How she loved him.

\* \* \*

It was late afternoon when Jared came back to the claim with a buggy. Jessie had insisted she keep the baby. Elizabeth leaned against Jared's strong arm as the buggy headed towards the banks of Cottonwood Creek. The trees waved their welcomes, their strong but feathery branches swayed in the Oklahoma breeze.

"Whoa." They stopped on the muddy bank and watched the brick–red water churn as it flowed over the sharp rocks.

Jared tied the horse to a tree branch and helped Elizabeth down. They found a log and sat in silence.

She must tell him.

He settled back, the scent of the wildflowers filling the air. Elizabeth felt safe, warm. How could she tell him? Jared spoke softly, telling her of his plans for the ranch, of settling his cattle, of building a soddy. Finally, he turned to her with that look in his eyes–just as he said, "Elizabeth."

She had blurted, "Jared."

"What?" he asked.

"What I began yesterday. I've got to tell you."

"About Hope's father."

"Yes."

"Are you sure? You don't have to tell me. That's your business."

"No, but it's now or never." She inhaled deeply. Another deep breath.

"I met William at my *debutante* ball. He was dashing, handsome, dressed in an Army uniform that flattered him. My aunt introduced us. I knew from her eyes that she approved of him. We danced, whispering polite replies to each other's nonsense. We danced for an hour and then he took me outside. I still remember how the stars shone on his thick blonde hair. He looked into my eyes and said, "You have captured me Miss Lee."

Elizabeth breathed in again, trying to draw courage from the Oklahoma air. Jared's hand squeezed her arm again. She bit a nail. "Then he kissed me. I should have known to be wary of him then, but he was handsome, and well, I was seventeen." She felt so much older now. How could this have all been just over eighteen months ago? She had grown a lifetime. "I kissed him back. We kissed for too long. I mixed up my excitement and somehow thought I was falling in love. From then on, he was at our house every night. My aunt and uncle welcomed him. His family had money. I'm sure they hoped he would marry me and take me off their hands."

Elizabeth paused and gazed at Jared out of the corner of her eye. His expression told her nothing as he stared at the backs of the horses. "I thought I was in love. He brought flowers and candy and then a diamond engagement ring. Then one night everything changed. I smelled liquor on him, but thought nothing of it. All men drink, right? Then one night my aunt and uncle were out of town. He came to supper. I didn't want him to, but he didn't listen to me. He was drunker than I had ever seen him."

The scenes ran together in her mind. She stopped talking and gulped, "He reeked of alcohol. He tried to kiss me, but I pulled away. He slapped my face." She touched the spot as if it still stung. "I turned and ran, and I guess he left."

"You told no one what happened?"

"No, who would have cared? My aunt would have told me I shouldn't have let him kiss me in the first place. Each time we were alone, he became increasingly violent. I avoided him. My Aunt Jane began planning the wedding. How could I get out of it? It was only six months away."

"Oh, Elizabeth."

She had to keep going or she would never finish. "I saw my uncle slap my aunt occasionally, so I figured that must be how men behaved. Until I met you. You respected me. No man had ever done that. Jared, you don't know what that means to me."

His eyes spoke what his words could not.

"One night he stayed late after everyone had gone to bed. I tried to slip away, claiming a headache, but he grabbed me–and then–he–I tried to scream but we were too far away from everyone. I hate huge houses. I tried to get away, but he pinned me to the floor."

Elizabeth shuddered. She felt sick "And then he–."

She sobbed. Suddenly. Violently. He drew her close. She cried on and on. Great wails from deep within her sent waves across the prairie grass. Somehow in her pain she recalled holding Jared as he cried that day over Aenohe. Elizabeth pulled herself from Jared's warm embrace.

"Oh, Elizabeth, I wish I could–" His fist punched his hand. "I could kill him for hurting you."

"Jared. . ."

"I know. What happened?"

"He went home. Came back two days later acting as if nothing happened. I don't think he even remembered. I didn't tell. It didn't happen again. He got drunk, but only pushed me around a little. Then I. . ."

"Figured out you were in the family way."

"Yes. I told no one. What could I do? I prayed I would lose it. You know the rest. I ran away and then we started towards Oklahoma."

"It's getting dark. We need to be getting back."

"We do."

He pulled her to her feet. Taking her face in his hands, his liquid green eyes sought her blues. With emotion in his voice he said, "Elizabeth, I love you." He kissed her gently, softly, his lips barely touching hers.

She took a deep breath and a step back.

"I just want you to know now. Whatever happened, it doesn't matter now. It's over. I'll take care of you. Will you let me take care of you and Hope forever?"

"But I just told you. . ."

"It doesn't matter. It's in the past. I love you."

"I want to. Oh, how I want to, but I'm so afraid."

"I'll wait until you are ready." They climbed into the buggy and headed back to the claim. He dropped her off, as she knew he could not stay inside after what had passed between them. He would probably sleep under the stars.

# 26

## *Love in the Heartland*

THE NEXT MORNING ELIZABETH tried to sort her emotions. Jessie was full of questions, but Elizabeth did not say much. It was Sunday and they were headed to church. She knew Jared would be there, and hopefully Emma, who might provide some advice and support.

Fortunately, she saw Emma, Sam, and all the children as soon as they entered the church. Jenny ran to her arms, with her voice running about their claim. Emma's strong hug renewed Elizabeth's strength. Elizabeth saw Aenohe sitting with Sam. He seemed to fit right in to Laverly family. So far there had been no trouble about his being Indian.

"Oh, Lizzie, how I've missed you. But our claim, it's beautiful, and Sam is plowing, and we are just so happy!"

"I'm so glad, Emma."

"What is it, girl? That look says you're up to something."

"Jared proposed."

"When's the wedding?"

"I just don't know." Unbeknownst to Elizabeth, Jared had approached the two. Elizabeth saw him walk away.

"Don't let him go." Emma pushed her out the church door after Jared. She rushed to catch up to him as he continued down the street.

"Jared!"

"What do you want? Have you made up your mind?" He swung around, boots scraping the boardwalk. "I never wanted anyone in my life, no one to get close to me. I had my horse and my cattle and that was enough. But since I met you, I want you in my life. I want to wake up every morning next to you. I want to see you riding across our land on this horse, the wind blowing through your hair. I want to have children with you—children to fill up the ranch house I want to build. I love you. Elizabeth, I need, I want an answer."

The beauty of his words hit her ears and soaked into her soul. She wanted him, yes, she wanted him.

"Yes."

The Oklahoma breeze blew just as it always would, and Jared's love, more powerful than the wind, drove all mistrust and fear to the far horizon.

# Epilogue

"Mama, thank you so much! I got the whole story on video!" Priscilla hugged her mother.

"Memaw, I love that story. I'm going to tell it to my children when I have them."

"That's what I want you to do, Lizzie Lou, tell your children, pass it down, so that no one forgets where we came from," said Anne.

"Did Lizzie and Jared get married?" asked Lizzie.

"The very next week, yes. Jared built Lizzie a soddy, in which they lived two years until he could build a better house. The house still stands, even though it is run down and no one lives there. I can show you next time we drive that way."

"Was Hope your mother?" Lizzie was trying to put all the pieces together.

"No, sweetie, my mother, the youngest of Jared and Lizzie's ten children, was born in 1908. Her name was Margaret Anne." "Your name is Margaret Anne, Memaw!" Lizzie exclaimed.

"Daddy named me after Mama, and they called me Anne."

"Some of your story sounds like fiction, Memaw, really, that lady jumped off the train and cowboys slid out the windows just to get land?" Lizzie asked.

"Oklahoma truth is stranger than fiction," laughed Anne.

"And the city of Guthrie was built over night? Why it took them a whole year just to build our house!"

"They were in a rush, Lizzie Lou, *a rush to the heartland.*"

Made in the USA
Columbia, SC
30 August 2021